D0354212

angels in pink

Raina's Story

You'll want to read these inspiring novels by

Lurlene McDaniel

One Last Wish novels

The Dawn Rochelle novels

Other fiction by Lurlene McDaniel

**From every ending
comes a new beginning....**

Lurlene McDaniel

angels in pink

Raina's Story

Delacorte  **Press**

I would like to express my gratitude to Jan Hamilton Powell and Mickey Milita of Erlanger Medical Center, Baroness campus, for their invaluable help in shaping this series.

Published by
Delacorte Press
an imprint of
Random House Children's Books
a division of Random House, Inc.
New York

Visit us on the Web! www.randomhouse.com/teens
Educators and librarians, for a variety of teaching tools, visit us at
www.randomhouse.com/teachers

Library of Congress Cataloging-in-Publication Data
McDaniel, Lurlene.
Raina's story / Lurlene McDaniel.
p.   cm. — (Angels in pink)
Summary: After sixteen-year-old Raina learns that she is a perfect match for donating bone marrow to a leukemia patient in Virginia, she discovers that the young woman is the sister she never knew she had.
ISBN 0-385-73157-4 (trade) — ISBN 0-385-90194-1 (GLB)
[1. Interpersonal relations—Fiction.   2. Mothers and daughters—Fiction.
3. Sisters—Fiction.   4. Leukemia—Fiction.   5. Friendship—Fiction.
6. Christian life—Fiction.   7. Florida—Fiction.   8. Virginia—Fiction.]
I. Title.
PZ7.M478172Rai 2005
[Fic]—dc22
2004010108

The text of this book is set in 11-point Goudy.

Book design by Michelle Gengaro

Printed in the United States of America

May 2005

10 9 8 7 6 5 4 3 2

BPT

This book is dedicated with love
to Conner Neal McDaniel.

Angels in Pink Volunteers' Creed

I will pass through this life but once.
If there is any kindness I can show, any good that I
can do, any comfort that I can offer, let me do it
now, for one day I will be gone and what
will remain is the memory of what I did for others.

one

"Is everything all right?" Raina St. James asked as soon as Kathleen McKensie had climbed into the car and shut the door.

"Sure," Kathleen said halfheartedly, turning her head so that Raina couldn't see her eyes filling with moisture. "Everything's fine. It's hard coming here, that's all." She had just toured the inside of her home while her friends waited for her in the car. She'd gone from room to room checking everything out, as she had every day for the past few weeks. Nothing was disturbed. Everything looked orderly and, except for some dust buildup, seemed the same as when she had been living there.

From the backseat, Holly Harrison reached out and patted Kathleen's shoulder. "Your mom won't be in the hospital forever. Didn't you say Dr. Kiefer was thinking of transferring her to the rehab center this week?"

Kathleen nodded, still gazing longingly out the car window at the front of her home. "It's just that I can't remember one time that my mom wasn't around for a first day of school. Ever since kindergarten."

"Well, we're here for you now, girlfriend," Raina said, backing her car out of the driveway.

"And . . . and I appreciate it," Kathleen said, finding a tissue and dabbing her eyes. She knew that Raina could have gone to school that morning with her boyfriend, Hunter, Holly's brother, but Raina had elected instead to face day one of their junior year with her best friends. Twisting in her seat, Kathleen told Holly, "And I know your mom tried hard to make the day special for us. It was nice of her to make waffles for breakfast because she knows I like them."

For the past several weeks, while her mother recovered from heart surgery, Kathleen had lived with Holly and her family. Because her father had died tragically years before, she and Mary Ellen had only each other. It had been fun being a part of Holly's family, but Kathleen was ready to go home. Only, her mother had weeks of rehabilitation to go through first, and Kathleen had to remain at Holly's.

"Mom lives to force-feed her family," Holly said, bulging her cheeks out in an exaggerated imitation of overeating. "I could have done just fine with cereal. The first day of school always makes me nervous, and when I'm nervous, I get sick to my stomach."

"Not in *my* car," Raina said, glancing in the rearview mirror at Holly. "Day one makes me excited," she added. "According to my schedule sheet, I can meet Hunter between three classes."

"Whoopee," Holly said without enthusiasm. "We get to meet him coming out of the bathroom every morning. Not a pretty sight."

This made Kathleen smile. "It's not that bad, Raina."

"And don't think I'm not jealous about it either." Raina was crazy about Hunter, now a senior at their high school, and she couldn't imagine facing the next year without him when he went off to college. "Speaking of boyfriends, what do you hear from Carson? I guess today's his first day too."

"He called last night," Kathleen said. "To wish me luck." Since Carson Kiefer attended the prestigious Bryce Academy on the other side of Tampa, she didn't expect to see him often. She figured it was only a matter of time before he forgot about her completely. Wasn't that what the nasty-tempered Stephanie Marlow had predicted to Kathleen at the end-of-the-year banquet for the Pink Angels hospital volunteers just a couple of weeks before?

The words buzzed in her memory. *"Don't think that just because he's fooled around with you all summer, I'm out of the picture. This has happened before, you know. He finds some new little plaything for a few months and keeps himself busy. But he always comes back to me."*

"Why don't you invite him to our first football game next Friday night? You can double with me and Hunter." Raina's voice pulled Kathleen into the present.

"Maybe I will. He told me he likes the two of you."

"Hey!" Holly interjected from the backseat. "What about me? Who will I go to the game with if you all double?"

"Is there anyone you could ask? We could make it a triple date," Raina said.

"As if my father will allow me to date anyone. I'll be an old dried-up prune before Dad ever lets go." Holly rolled her eyes. Mike Harrison was known for his strictness, especially when it came to Holly. Since she was the youngest of her friends and wouldn't be sixteen until mid-May, she knew she was facing another dateless year. "Is it going to be like this all year?" she groused. "You two running off on dates and me sitting home all alone?"

"We still have our volunteer jobs at the hospital," Raina offered. "We'll be together then."

"And don't think I'm not glad about it, but that's only two afternoons a week."

"And on Saturdays, if you want. I know I'm going to volunteer most Saturdays," Raina said. Hunter worked on Saturdays at a fast-food place, so she'd already decided to volunteer at the hospital while he was busy, because it allowed her to miss him less. "What do you say?"

"Count me in," Holly said, still unhappy about her solo status. "Anything's better than hanging around the house being bored and getting into my parents' way."

"I don't think I can commit," Kathleen said. "At least not until Mom's home and I see what her needs are going to be." Even before Carson's father had performed heart surgery on Mary Ellen, Kathleen had hesitated to be away from her mother too long. Because Mary Ellen was a victim of multiple sclerosis and Kathleen was her primary caregiver, much of her mother's care fell on Kathleen's shoulders.

"Well, don't let her tie you down too much," Raina said in a lecturing tone. "You're just now getting a real life."

"Raina . . ." Kathleen's voice held a warning note.

"Just a caution," Raina added quickly. By now they were in front of the high school, and she whipped the car into the student parking lot, which was already filling with returning students' vehicles. "I have to go to the office and get a parking permit for this school year," she announced.

"I'll come with you," Kathleen said.

"I'm casing out the commons," Holly said. "I'll meet you there before first bell"—she looked at her watch—"say, in twenty minutes." They'd purposefully left extra early so that they could hang in the school's large atrium to check out incoming freshmen and hook up with old friends.

"If I can get the permit in twenty minutes, that's where we'll meet. Tell Hunter to wait with you, okay?"

"As if he'll stand around with his sister." Holly snorted.

They piled out of the car, gathering up their purses, new notebooks and supplies. Three big yellow school buses were lined in front of the auditorium, and kids were off-loading. Cummings High was less than ten years old, well planned and shaped much like a huge wheel, with the atrium at its hub and classrooms shooting off like spokes. The grades were kept in separate wings, so that except for assemblies and pep rallies, kids moved through with their own class. The student body was large and it was easy to get lost in the throngs, but Raina and Kathleen knew their way around, so they sidestepped the crowds and headed toward the office wing.

"I hope this won't take forever," Raina grumbled as they hurried. "I really want to see Hunter before the bell rings."

"What are you going to do when he goes off to college?"

"Mourn."

Kathleen laughed. "Maybe you can test out and go to college with him a year early."

"Holly's the smart one, remember? I'll need every minute to keep my grades steady."

"Then you should be relieved that you won't have any distractions next year."

"Are you kidding? I'm worried that my lips will dry up and fall off from lack of kissing."

"He *will* come home on breaks," Kathleen said with a grin.

As they walked, Kathleen couldn't help noticing that Raina waved and nodded to half the population in the halls. She seemed to know everyone. And why not? Raina was pretty and popular. That was the way it had always been. Holly, cute and perky. Kathleen, shy and quiet. How she had ever attracted Carson was still a mystery to her. And even if they didn't last— *please God, let us last*—she was facing her junior year feeling like a veteran of the dating wars. Through the summer, she'd had a wonderful time with a totally awesome guy, thanks to the hospital volunteer program where she'd first met Carson.

"Here we are," Raina said, looking dismayed at the line snaking from the main office. A second later, she perked up. Along the hallway, a table had been set up, and behind the table sat a teacher. Above him, taped to the wall, was a sign that read

PARKING PERMITS. UPPERCLASSMEN ONLY. "Can they possibly be this organized? I'm stunned."

"Go get your permit. I'll wait over here," Kathleen said, stepping out of the stream of foot traffic. She leaned against the wall, wondering how Carson's first day was going. Bryce Academy took Tampa's elite and wealthy, so it probably wasn't as chaotic as Cummings. She longed to hear his voice, see his face. Yet for all his attentions, Kathleen still felt insecure. He could have any girl he wanted. Why had he chosen her? She wasn't beautiful like Stephanie, who also attended Bryce. Stephanie was a model, and her pictures were all over newspapers and magazines. Kathleen caught sight of herself in the plate glass of the case across the hall that housed the school's sports and academic trophies. Her long red hair looked frizzy with the humidity and her shirt was droopy. Maybe it *was* better that Carson went to another school after all and couldn't see her at the moment.

"Got it." Raina waved the permit and decal at Kathleen. "Let's go hook up with Holly."

Kathleen fished for her class schedule as they walked. "Umm, it says here that I have geometry first period. How about you?"

"English lit. Lunch at twelve-forty."

"I'll miss you by fifteen minutes."

"Last period on Tuesdays and Thursdays are our volunteer times. We can meet in the parking lot and all go together. And don't forget—orientation's this Saturday morning. I'll pick you and Holly up. You going to break out of Admissions and record filing?"

"I like it there. No blood." Kathleen wasn't crazy about hospitals, so remaining in the admissions office and working with paper and files seemed logical to her.

"Just remember, we're getting a school credit this time around, so diversity counts." For Raina, the credit was an unexpected bonus. She'd have worked without it, but the Pink Angels program offered a high school credit if a student volunteered a hundred and sixty hours a semester. A volunteer could work more hours if he or she had a parent on staff. Raina's mother, Vicki, was director of nursing, so Raina already knew she'd be at the hospital beyond the requirement for credit.

"The difference between us," Kathleen said, "is that you want a career in medicine, while I just want to graduate from high school and get into a decent college. I volunteer to be with my friends."

Raina sighed. "You're just too honest."

"What's this?" Kathleen asked, seeing Holly barreling toward them, dodging clusters of students along the way. Her face looked pinched and pale, and she was clutching her notebook to her chest with a death grip.

Holly stopped short in front of Raina and grabbed her arm. "Don't go to the atrium."

"Why? What's wrong?"

"You look like you've seen a ghost," Kathleen said.

"Worse than a ghost." Holly's voice trembled. "I've seen the devil himself." She looked Raina in the eye. "I—I'm sorry to have to tell you this, Raina, but Tony Stoddard's back."

two

RAINA'S STOMACH LURCHED as if she'd just fallen twenty stories in an out-of-control elevator. *Tony Stoddard.* The one person who could ruin her life. "Are you sure?"

Holly nodded and scowled. "Oh, he's older and more beefed up and his hair's longer, but it's the same old Tony. He's in the commons now, bragging and greeting all his old friends from middle school. Seems they still remember him."

"I thought he was gone forever." Kathleen sounded dismayed.

"I guess not," Raina said, her heart thudding with dread.

"I overheard him saying his father got reassigned to McDill." Holly named the big air force base in Tampa where Tony's father had served when they were in middle school together. "How can the air force do that to you?"

Raina offered a wan smile. "I'm sure they didn't single me out."

"I don't think we should go down to the commons," Kathleen said. "It's a big school. Maybe you won't run into each other."

"For the whole year? Unlikely," Raina said. Hunter's image leaped into her mind. "Oh no . . . what about Hunter?"

Holly shook her head. "He never knew Tony. Remember, Hunter was here at Cummings in ninth grade while we were still in eighth."

Raina hadn't begun dating Hunter until she was a sophomore at Cummings and Hunter was a junior.

Holly continued. "And since Hunter's a senior now, I don't think he'll travel in the same circles as Tony. Why would he?"

"Plus, you've already told us that he's really busy with his job at the burger place, and of course, busy with schoolwork and *you*," Kathleen reminded Raina.

"It's nice of the two of you to help me feel better about this. Truth is, it's hard to keep a secret in this school and you know it. I'm just going to keep a low profile and hope for the best."

Kathleen didn't see how that was possible, because Raina was so popular, but she kept her opinion to herself.

"Sounds like a good plan," Holly said. "Besides, maybe Tony's forgotten what happened. I mean, it *did* happen in eighth grade."

"Years ago," Kathleen said enthusiastically.

Raina smiled politely, but they all knew they didn't believe it. Not for a minute.

On Saturday, Raina picked up her friends and they all reported to Parker-Sloan General Hospital for orientation about their upcoming volunteer duties for high school credit. They had gone through an orientation at the beginning of the summer, but this time it was different. There would be little leeway for skipping days, tighter controls on their work, and supervisory reports filled out and turned in to their high school. The room where this orientation was held was much smaller than the teaching auditorium from the summer. As they took their seats, Raina recognized a few faces from the summer program but saw new people too. In all, she estimated that about sixty kids had signed up from schools all over the city.

Connie, the coordinator from the summer program, greeted everyone warmly, then introduced a petite young woman named Sierra Benson, the coordinator for the credit program as part of a work-study exchange. She was a senior at the University of South Florida seeking a degree in medical community relations. More and more hospitals needed good PR, according to Raina's mother. "Hospitals are businesses," Vicki sometimes grumbled. "I wish it wasn't so much that way, but it is."

Still, Raina had her heart set on becoming a nurse herself, despite her mother's flagging enthusiasm for her own career as the years passed and her profession faced ever-changing challenges. Raina considered her summer as a Pink Angel, and now her for-credit sign-up, as one step closer to fulfilling her dream.

"Hello," Sierra said with a smile. "I'm really looking forward to working with all of you. Let me begin by saying that I want us to be friends as well as colleagues. I want you to come to me with any concerns about your work and your schedules and your supervisors—in short, come to me about anything. This is going to be a good year and with your help, we'll build the most successful high school volunteer program in Parker-Sloan's history."

"She doesn't look much older than us," Holly whispered to her friends.

Sierra went on to explain the rules and routines. She passed out paperwork and told them that the new assignment room would be next to the medical library. "While you're on duty, you'll each be given a pager for use in the hospital. You'll check it in and out each day, and when it buzzes, go to an in-house phone and call your supervisor. Some of you will be assigned to the same nursing unit for weeks at a time. Some will be assigned to a resident during his or her specific rotation, and you'll be totally available to help them, run errands for them, whatever. Any questions?'"

"My very own resident. *That* sounds like fun," Holly whispered.

"I was hoping to stay in Admissions," Kathleen mumbled.

"Spread your wings," Raina urged softly.

Kathleen made a face.

When the orientation was over, Raina led her friends up to meet Sierra.

"Are you related to Vicki St. James?" Sierra asked after the introductions.

"My mom."

"I like her."

"Me too." Raina often thought of her mother as a best friend.

Sierra smiled. "I've looked over the comment sheets from the summer program, and everyone you all worked with gave you high marks. Congratulations."

"I—I really like Admissions," Kathleen ventured.

"I'm going to be moving people around," Sierra said. "By reading the comment sheets and talking to various supervisors, I think I can fit skills and personalities better."

Kathleen was disappointed, but she kept it to herself.

"Then we'll see you Tuesday," Raina said.

Holly kept up a running stream of conversation as they walked to Raina's car in the parking garage, but when they arrived at the vehicle, Carson Kiefer stepped out from behind a concrete pillar. "Hey, beautiful," he said to Kathleen.

"What are you doing here?" Her mood shot straight up.

"Seeing you. How'd the orientation go?"

"Fine. Wish you were signed up."

He shrugged. "I've got to get my grades up. I need to focus. That's hard to do when I'm around you."

"Uh—why don't we wait for you in my car," Raina said, nudging Holly.

"Better yet, why don't I take you home," Carson said. "I mean, take you to Holly's house. We'll grab a burger first."

Kathleen looked at her friends. "I'm sure you won't miss me."

"We'll cope," Raina teased.

Kathleen took Carson's hand, and Raina and Holly watched them walk away. Holly sighed heavily. "Wish I had a boyfriend."

"Does Carson seem more serious-minded to you?" Raina asked.

"What do you mean? He's serious about Kathleen, I think."

"I know. But ever since the night he resuscitated Kathleen's mother, he's seemed less like the party guy we first met."

"I haven't noticed. Whenever he calls her, I leave the room so they can have privacy. I'm such a good girl."

"Come on," Raina said with a laugh. "Hunter said he'll be off at five and if I hang around your house, I can be there when he arrives."

"Well, doesn't that work out nicely," Holly grumbled.

"Oh now, don't be a grouch. We can go shopping first if you'd like."

"Mom's got a list of chores for me to do."

"I'll help you."

"Really?"

Raina looped her arm through Holly's. "Really. We could become sisters-in-law someday, you know."

"Really?"

"Really."

"I missed you today," Raina whispered in Hunter's ear.

They were on an old blanket in a wooded area on the grounds of her town house complex, one of the few places where they could be alone together. She was wrapped in his arms, and his mouth was pressed against her throat. The night air felt warm and sticky, slick with the promise of

September rain. Pale light from the moon flickered through the branches of overhead trees, dripping with Spanish moss.

"Same for me," he said. "I'm crazy busy at my job, but I still have time to think about you. About us."

She was cradled against the length of his body, every one of her nerve endings on fire for him. "*Us*. I like the sound of it."

He kissed her, long and deep, and the taste of him was so familiar that she could have kissed a hundred others blindfolded and still known his mouth. Her head swam with passion and every inch of her skin tingled. No matter how many times they kissed, she always wanted more of him. "What about us?" she asked when he broke away.

"That it's getting harder and harder to be alone with you and . . . and not . . ." He didn't complete the sentence.

Her heart hammered inside her chest as if it wanted to break free. "I—I know," she said. She would have given him anything he asked of her. *Anything.* "I love you, Hunter."

He buried his face between her breasts, ran his hands down the long arc of her body rising to meet his caress. "And I love you."

She thought she might die from longing for him. There was only him. He was all she wanted. All she had ever wanted. "It's . . . okay. . . . ," she said. "I . . . want . . . us to . . ."

His hands stopped moving. She felt his body tense, and his slow, languid kisses ceased. A sound halfway between a moan and a growl escaped his throat. He pulled away, sat up very straight, grabbed his knees and pulled them tightly against his chest. "We can't, Raina," he said dully. "We just can't."

three

RAINA QUICKLY TUGGED at her clothing, sat up and scooted next to Hunter. "I—I'm sorry. I lost my head and forgot about the Promise."

Hunter turned toward her and shards of moonlight glanced across the planes of his face. He looked haunted, wounded. "You have nothing to be sorry about. It's *my* promise. I'm the one who has to keep it. We shouldn't have come here."

She took a deep shuddering breath, trying to calm her racing heart and douse the fire of passion still roaring through her veins. Years before, at a church camp, Hunter had pledged to remain chaste until he married. Raina had always known this, and it had been one of the things that had attracted her to him. Hunter wasn't like other boys she'd dated, who often figured they were entitled to have sex with her simply because they were dating. The irony was that she would have given herself to Hunter gladly because she loved him so much. And although they didn't share the same religious beliefs—she rarely went to church, while Hunter and his family attended faithfully—she respected his.

Raina said, "We hardly ever get to be alone, Hunter, and I wanted us to be alone."

"And now we know why we shouldn't be alone."

She stood abruptly. "Look, I didn't mean to get us to the edge of a meltdown by coming out here. I don't want you feeling bad about us. Besides, we seem to always be able to stop before . . . well, before we go too far."

He rose quickly and took her by the arms. "What scares me is what if I'm not able to stop? I don't want us to give ourselves away to each other on some blanket in the woods. I want it to be right when it happens. I want to be married."

"To me?"

"Of course to you. We love each other and we should be willing to declare it in front of God, and our families and friends. Then we can have all the sex we want, wherever we want."

"Aren't there rules about 'wherever'?" She attempted to lighten the mood.

He kissed the tip of her nose. "Yes. We'll be very careful to stay out of public elevators."

Looking into his eyes, she knew that his way did seem best, but it could be years before they would be able to marry. She said so to him, adding, "In the meantime, what are we supposed to do? Break up? Burn up? Dry up?"

A smile turned up the corners of his mouth, and he put his arms around her and pulled her close. "No to all three. We just have to stay in crowds, I guess. Do you think we can do that?"

She nodded, feeling hollow. "Just so long as we don't give up."

"That won't happen."

"No matter what?"

"What matters is doing things right," he said. "It's important to me, you know it is."

"I know," she said, holding him tightly, while an overwhelming sadness swept through her that she could not explain. Not to her own heart. Not to him.

Hunter told her goodbye at her front door, and Raina slunk inside. To her surprise, her mother was sitting at the countertop that jutted into the great room, poring over a pile of paperwork. Vicki looked up. Her eyes narrowed. "You all right? You looked bedraggled."

Raina had hoped to get up the stairs and into her room and wished she hadn't run into her mother. "Why are you up so late?"

"Catching up on reports I can't get to at work." Vicki laid down her pen. "Have you been with Hunter?"

"None other." Raina dropped the old blanket

on the floor and headed toward the refrigerator. She had no reason to be secretive now.

"Raina, you are being careful, aren't you?"

"*Hunter's* being careful," Raina said, retrieving an apple from the fruit bin and shutting the door. "I'd go for the gold if it was up to me."

"Don't say that. Teenage pregnancy is no joking matter."

"Why are you forever warning me about not getting pregnant? Don't forget, I got my very own prescription of birth control pills when I was fourteen. Why, I was the first girl in school to receive such a thoughtful gift. And from my mother too." Raina bit into the apple, well aware of how sarcastic she sounded. She didn't know why she was being hateful. It wasn't her mother's fault that she felt frustrated.

Vicki's mouth formed a thin, tight line. "That was for your own protection. Do you think some guy is going to stop in the middle of everything and take precautions?"

"Hunter isn't 'some guy.' He's a *perfect* guy."

Vicki arched her eyebrow. "In other words, he's not a loser, like your father, the guy *I* picked."

"I didn't say that."

"But you were thinking it."

That was the trouble with having a mother who was so much like her, Raina thought. They had no secrets from each other. "Well, he didn't stick around, did he?"

Vicki returned to the stool and her stack of papers. "No, he didn't. But I assure you, we're a whole lot better off without him."

"So you've always said."

Vicki pulled her reading glasses from where she had positioned them atop her head and set them on her nose. "Go to bed, Raina. I'm really too tired to spar with you tonight."

Raina teetered indecisively, her bad mood morphing into one of remorse. Her mother had worked hard and long to achieve her goals, all the while raising Raina alone without financial or emotional help from the father who'd walked out when Raina had been two. "Mom, I'm sorry," she said softly.

Vicki looked up. "I know. Trust me, I'm not keeping score, Raina. I'm glad we can talk to each other about anything. So many women on staff at the hospital tell me real horror stories about their relationships with their daughters." She blew out a breath. "I want your life to be better than mine. Easier. You'll want the same thing for your kids someday."

Raina dropped her half-eaten apple in the garbage can, walked out into the great room and flipped on the TV with the remote. She sank into the couch and surfed until she found *Saturday Night Live*.

"Why don't you go on to bed?" Vicki said.

"I'll wait for you."

Vicki closed the file she was working on and shoved it aside. "My eyes are crossing." She opened the pantry, found a bag of popcorn and put it into the microwave, then came and sat beside Raina on the sofa. "Can I watch with you?"

"Sure."

They settled into the cushions, one on each end of the pillow-strewn sofa, while the bag of popcorn exploded in the oven and the homey aroma of fresh buttery kernels filled the room.

On Labor Day, Kathleen went over to Carson's house, on Davis Island, for a barbecue around the pool with his parents. She remembered the first time she had gone there for dinner and how scared she'd been of the two heart surgeons, but now they seemed like old friends, and not only because Dr. Chris Kiefer had saved her mother's life. Kathleen genuinely liked Carson's parents. Carson's mother, Dr. Teresa, as Kathleen called her, was open and warm, with a great deal of charm and grace. Kathleen felt at ease around her.

Kathleen was lounging in the bright aqua water on a hot pink float when Carson rose up and grabbed the side of the float. "Yikes, don't dunk me," she said. "I just put on sunscreen."

His brown eyes glinted with mischief and the sun danced across his tanned shoulders. He slung water off his dark hair. "It'll cost you."

"What?" She eyed him warily.

"How about a kiss?"

"Your parents are watching us," Kathleen hissed.

"I'm sure they suspect that we kiss each other."

Kathleen felt her face getting red. Teresa was sitting on a lounger at the far end of the pool reading a medical journal. Carson's father was busy basting something that smelled succulent on the mammoth grill under the porch awning. "I'd be too embarrassed," she said.

"We can't have you embarrassed," Carson said, wiggling the float.

"Carson, don't!"

But her plea was in vain. With a heave, Carson turned the float over and Kathleen tumbled into the cool water. In a second, he was underwater beside her. He pulled her close and kissed her. She came up sputtering. "Resistance is futile," he said.

She splashed him full in the face. He laughed, arched backward and dove under. Kathleen swam to the side of the pool and raised herself out of the water. Teresa smiled and waved her over. "Men are little children. Why they think it is funny to partially drown their girlfriends is a mystery, but they all do. When Christopher first dated me, he did the same thing." She handed Kathleen a fluffy white towel.

"It's all about the hair," Kathleen confessed. "It just dries weird."

"Your hair is lovely. You should not fight it so."

"That's what my mother says."

"How is she doing? I know that medically she is doing well, but I mean otherwise."

"She is *so* ready to come home. And . . . and I really want her to." Unbidden, tears welled up in Kathleen's eyes. She dabbed them away with the edge of the towel. "I'm sorry."

Teresa patted Kathleen's arm. "No apologies. It is good to miss your mother. I still miss mine, although she died years ago."

"Mom has a nice room at the rehab center," Kathleen said, regaining her composure. "She goes to therapy twice a day. I think things would go faster if it weren't for her MS."

The facility where Mary Ellen was staying was a block away from Parker-Sloan. It had one wing for patients who needed therapy but couldn't yet live alone at home, a pool for water exercises and several large gymlike rooms filled with equipment. Physical therapists on staff worked with both inpatients and outpatients. Many who went there were victims of strokes and accidents. Kathleen could see that her mother was getting better every day but that she still had a way to go before being allowed to return home. Even when she did, Mary Ellen would have to return for therapy twice a week.

Kathleen said, "Mom's attitude is better . . . more positive."

"Well, certainly repairing her heart valve improved blood flow, and this gave her more energy," Teresa said. "She was truly very sick."

Kathleen thought that her mother's close brush with death had somehow strengthened her, helped her see beyond her illness and the terrible loss of her husband and Kathleen's father in a car wreck years before. "She's better now. In a lot of ways," Kathleen said.

"Hey, watch this!" Carson called from the diving board.

Kathleen and Teresa turned to see Carson execute a perfect dive into the sparkling water. A feeling of contentment spread through Kathleen. She cared about Carson more than she admitted to him, and spending time with him and his family gave her a sense of belonging.

A noise at the side gate and Dr. Kiefer calling out "Hello there" from his position at the grill made Kathleen swivel around and shield her eyes from the sun. Her heart skipped a beat and her stomach fell to her toes. Coming through the yard and across the brick patio toward them was none other than her nemesis, the beautiful Stephanie Marlow.

four

STEPHANIE CLAPPED when Carson surfaced and then went straight over to Teresa's chair, bent and kissed her on the cheek. They greeted each other warmly in Spanish while Kathleen sank lower into her lounge chair.

"Have you met Kathleen?" Teresa asked.

Stephanie gave Kathleen a cursory glance. "Carson's little friend. Yes, we've met," she said, then turned her back to Kathleen.

Little friend? Kathleen felt her cheeks grow hot and her temper flare.

Kathleen listened as Teresa and Stephanie carried on a conversation in fluent Spanish. If awards for rudeness were passed out, Stephanie would win one hands down. It seemed obvious to her that Stephanie was flaunting her language expertise to show Kathleen up, for Kathleen understood very little Spanish and couldn't speak much of it outside of ordering tacos at a restaurant.

Carson's father strolled over holding a tray

with several choices of soft drinks. "Want one?" he asked the three of them.

Kathleen took a can of diet cola, and so did Stephanie. Carson swam laps in the pool, making Kathleen assume that he didn't want to face both of them just yet. *Coward!*

"How are your parents?" Dr. Kiefer asked.

"Dad's in Switzerland on business. Mom's in Brazil." Stephanie didn't elaborate.

"Are you staying alone?" Dr. Teresa asked, in a tone that made Kathleen wonder if she might invite Stephanie to stay over for a few days.

"The housekeeper and the cook are there. So is the groundskeeper. I have company. And I have school. And"—Stephanie flashed a smile— "I have friends."

Gag me, Kathleen thought, hoping it didn't show in her expression.

"You must stay for dinner," Teresa said. "There's plenty because Chris always cooks for an army."

Kathleen's stomach knotted. This wasn't the way she wanted to spend the evening.

"Absolutely," Carson's father said.

"I'd like to stay. Thank you."

Carson pulled himself out of the water and padded over. To Kathleen's dismay, he chose to stand next to his father and not beside her chair. She longed to have him put his hands on her shoulders in a possessive gesture that would speak volumes to Stephanie. "What's up?" he asked.

"Burned meat if I don't take it off the grill," Dr. Kiefer said.

"I'll help," Carson said.

"I have some salads inside," Teresa said, getting up from her lounger. "I'll bring them out to the table."

"Let me help," Kathleen said, pushing up from her chair.

Beside her, Stephanie popped the top on her can of cola and a plume of sticky spray gushed all over Kathleen's face and hair. "Oh, goodness!" Stephanie cried. "So sorry."

Everyone turned to stare, and Kathleen went red with anger and embarrassment. She knew it was no accident, recalling how Stephanie had been turning the can over and over to build up pressure while she talked to the Kiefers. Cola dripped off Kathleen's nose and forehead. Teresa grabbed up a towel and fussed over Kathleen, who took the towel and forced a smile. "No harm done. I was going to take a quick swim before going inside." She started toward the pool.

"Then I'll help you bring out the food," Stephanie said to Carson's mother brightly.

Kathleen dove into the cool water, certain that steam would rise from her skin, she was so mad. She held her breath for a long time, until her lungs felt as if they would burst, and wondered if anyone would even notice if she *never* came up.

"You're sure quiet tonight," Carson said. He was driving Kathleen to Holly's house. They were almost there and had hardly spoken a word during the trip from Davis Island to the other side of town.

"Not much to say." She was brooding. Stephanie had remained at Carson's house through dinner and a movie in the Kiefers' state-of-the-art home theater. In fact, she seemed perfectly at home in the grand house, and Kathleen was left to wonder how many times Stephanie had been inside Carson's bedroom suite adjoining the theater. Kathleen had seen it only once, but she'd never forget the silver-framed photo of Stephanie. Kathleen had tried to outlast Stephanie, but finally she had to leave because of school the next day.

"Look, I'm sorry Steffie horned in on the day. It's not like I invited her, if that's what you're thinking," Carson said.

"Yes, poor Steffie . . . all alone on Labor Day."

"What's with you and her? I don't get why you don't like her." He sounded irritated.

"Well, there was the cola incident. That didn't endear her to me one bit."

He blew air through his lips. By now they

had arrived at Holly's. He shoved the car into park, but before Kathleen could jump out, he pushed the door lock down. "Let's talk."

"I'd rather go inside."

"Not yet. I need to explain a few things about Steffie."

"Not interested." But of course, she was.

He ignored her protest. "She doesn't have many girlfriends."

"That's a surprise. Could it be because she's such a . . . a . . ." Kathleen stopped short of using the word she wanted to use.

"Will you just listen?" Carson said sharply.

"Do I have a choice?" Kathleen crossed her arms.

"Steffie's had a pathetic home life. In spite of the maids and cooks," he added before Kathleen could say anything sarcastic. "Her father's always away on business. He runs a furniture importing enterprise and it made him rich, but absent. Her mother is Brazilian and from some kind of wealthy political family down there. She's very beautiful and was once a runner-up in a Miss USA contest before she got married."

That explained where Stephanie got her looks, Kathleen thought, but not her personality.

"We were in the same sixth-grade class together and she was the loneliest kid I'd ever met. My mom started bringing her home to our house every day after school so she wouldn't be alone.

Steffie's mother never seemed to mind where Steffie went. That is, whenever her mother was at home. She hates living in the U.S. and is always running back to Brazil. When Steffie's parents are together, they fight like cats and dogs."

"Why don't they just get divorced?"

In the darkened car, she saw Carson shrug. "I think they enjoy making each other miserable. And Steffie's always been their weapon of choice, if you know what I mean. Anyway, my parents sort of took Steffie in through middle school. The only time her mother showed any real interest in Steffie was when she went into modeling. My mom argued against it but lost. Steffie was only thirteen."

"It's obvious that she's pretty," Kathleen said grudgingly.

"And when they dress her for a photo shoot, she looks twenty-five."

"Boys fall all over her."

"Why do you think that's a good thing?"

She had no quick answer. He was a boy and he couldn't understand how important it was to girls to be noticed and liked by boys. The porch light flashed. "That's Holly's father telling me I've been parked out here in the dark long enough." Instead of feeling resentment, she felt relieved. She was weary of hearing about Stephanie. And while Carson might feel sorry for Stephanie, Kathleen didn't.

"Holly's right—the man's a dictator," Carson said grudgingly.

"Holly exaggerates. He's just overprotective. He worries about me as much as he does her."

Carson shook his head. "Well, I wouldn't want to sully your reputation. Come on, I'll walk you to the door." He unlocked the car doors and they walked to the porch. "Do you have a better understanding about Steffie now and how she fits into my life?" he asked at the stoop.

Not one bit, Kathleen thought. "I guess so," she said. But as she slipped into the house, all she could think about was that he was going back home, and she'd bet a week's worth of hall passes that Stephanie would be waiting for him.

"Why are guys so dense? Why don't they catch on to the games girls play?" Kathleen was draped across Holly's bed later that night, still stewing over Carson and Stephanie. Holly was sitting on the floor carefully applying glittery decals to her newly painted purple fingernails.

"How should I know? I have no experience with boys, remember?"

"Is Carson blind? Can't he see how Stephanie feels about him?" Kathleen rolled over and stared up at the ceiling, her long red hair trailing onto the floor.

"Maybe he doesn't want to see. Raina says guys play games too . . . you know, pit one girl against another." Holly looked up, her eyes widening. "Sorry, I shouldn't have said that."

Kathleen sighed and her heart gave a tug. "I couldn't stand it if Carson was playing games with me."

"Carson likes you, Kathleen, or he wouldn't keep coming back."

"You think?"

"Of course, I—" Holly was interrupted by a knock on her bedroom door.

"It's Dad." Mike Harrison's voice sounded through the wood. Kathleen sat upright and Holly scrambled to put away her polish and decals. The door opened and Mike stuck his head into the room. His grin faded when he saw Holly's nails. "What's this?"

Boldly, Holly held out her hands. "The newest look. All the girls are wearing it."

"I don't see Kathleen's hands painted like a streetwalker's."

Holly flushed crimson. "Dad! That's not a nice thing to say."

"Take it off."

"But Dad—"

"No buts. I'll inspect tomorrow at breakfast." He nodded at Kathleen. "Did you have a good time with Carson's family?"

"Yes." She almost trembled. The man wasn't even her father, yet his authority was unquestionable. "We had a cookout by the pool, then watched a movie." She skipped the part about Stephanie crashing the cookout.

"Good." He smiled. "You two go on to bed and I'll see you in the morning." He shut the door and Holly threw a pillow at it.

"He makes me crazy!" Holly all but shouted. "Why can't I have painted purple nails? What's wrong with purple nails?"

Kathleen tugged on her nightshirt. She should tell Holly that the nails were really ugly and that her father had done her a favor, but why start an argument? She climbed into the trundle bed and pulled the covers up while Holly slammed around the bedroom. Her thoughts returned to Carson and Stephanie, and she remembered that Raina also had often said that there was a fine line between acting like a possessive, jealous shrew and watching out for what was yours. *"Smart girls learn how to walk that line, because guys can't stand girls with strangleholds. But girls who don't watch their turf can lose it."*

Kathleen didn't want to lose Carson to Stephanie, but she didn't want to scare him off either. She punched her pillow in frustration and rolled over to face the wall.

"Do you have to hit every bump in the parking lot?" Holly was furiously applying a coat of purple polish to her fingernails in the backseat of Raina's car.

"Can't you do your manicures at night?" Raina asked.

Kathleen said nothing about the edict from Holly's father.

Raina pulled into a parking space. "Besides, we have to go to the hospital today, and you can't wear that stuff around the patients. Read your rules."

"I know," Holly said. "And I'll take it off on the way this afternoon. But for today—" She held up her finished nails and admired them. "They looked better with the decals."

They were halfway to the side door when Raina said, "Crud! I forgot my chem book in the trunk."

"We'll wait for you," Kathleen said just as the first bell rang.

"No, you'll be late. Go on. I'll meet you at the car at one-thirty." Raina rushed back to the car, retrieved her book, slammed the trunk and hurried to the building. She was about to pull open the door when it flew open for her. "I thought that was you," a boy said, his grin more a sneer than a smile.

Her stomach tied into knots. She was looking up at the face of Tony Stoddard.

five

"Why, Raina, you don't look happy to see me," Tony said. "It's your old friend, Tony. Don't tell me you don't remember."

"Some things I'd rather forget," she said, attempting to brush past him. Three of his friends stood behind him, reminding her of wolves waiting for the kill.

"And I thought we had something special going," Tony said.

"That was a long time ago."

"But I'm back now." He threw open his arms, and his friends grunted out laughs.

"I have a boyfriend." She tried to pass him again, but he blocked her.

"So I've heard. A senior. But I'm not impressed."

"He's worth three of you, Tony."

One of his friends groaned. "Ow, knife to your heart, Tony, my man."

Tony's eyes narrowed. "You didn't think that way when we were in eighth grade."

It struck her that Tony, whom she disliked,

knew exactly what her body looked like without clothes. And Hunter, whom she loved, did not. She felt humiliated by the thought, and just the memory of Tony's hands on her made her skin crawl. "I was stupid back then. Now I know the difference between someone who really cares and someone who fakes it."

Tony's friends hooted and Tony glowered, malevolence all but shooting from his eyes.

"Shouldn't you all be in class?" The teacher's voice startled them and made the group of boys jump backward.

Raina was never so grateful to see a teacher in her life. "On my way," she said, this time brushing by Tony.

"This isn't over," he hissed as she passed.

She ignored him, but her whole body was icy cold. She believed his threat and felt sickened. Her one hope was that Hunter loved her more than Tony hated her.

Raina told Kathleen and Holly about her encounter on the way to the hospital.

"The guy's a creep," Kathleen said.

"Want me to sic my father on him?" Holly asked. "Nobody stands up to my dad." She said it with a kind of pride that surprised Raina because Holly groused about her father so much.

"What's he going to do? Break Tony's knees?"

"Something wrong with that?"

Raina laughed for the first time that day. "I wish it were that simple. It's Tony's mouth that needs breaking."

"What *are* you going to do?" Kathleen asked.

"I don't know," Raina said. "I really don't know."

She was still stewing over her problem when they arrived at the Pink Angels volunteer room headquarters, where Sierra greeted them. "Why, it's the Three Musketeers. Are you ready to jump into deep water?"

"How deep?" Kathleen was worried.

"You're an excellent worker, Kathleen. You've gotten wonderful reviews, but I realize you'd rather work with paper than with patients. Therefore, you're being assigned next door, to the medical library, and the librarian is your supervisor."

"Really?" The assignment suited Kathleen just fine.

"And me?" Holly asked.

"Children's ward. I've been told that you're Mrs. Graham's favorite art director."

Holly had to laugh because she'd managed to spill more paint than help kids who were recovering from illnesses and accidents apply it to paper.

"And me?" Raina asked. "Where are you placing me?"

"The newborn nursery, up in ob-gyn."

"Babies? I get to help with the babies?" She couldn't have been more delighted.

Sierra laughed. "When they're all crying at once, they make quite a racket. Some of the nurses actually wear earplugs." She handed each girl a routing sheet. "Have your supervisors sign these and return them to me at the end of each shift. And don't forget your pagers."

The girls fastened the pagers to their belts, grabbed their paperwork and headed for their assignments. "See you at my car at five," Raina called, speeding off, her problems with Tony momentarily forgotten.

On the ob/gyn floor, she reported to her immediate supervisor, Ms. Betsy Kohn, a tall, attractive woman wearing the uniform of her ward—green slacks and a pale yellow top sprinkled with images of cuddly bunnies and fuzzy baby chicks. She wore a stethoscope around her neck and had several pacifiers safety-pinned to her breast pocket. "You come to appreciate these things," Betsy told Raina, gesturing to the tiny pacifiers. "The person who invented them should be nominated for sainthood. Come on. I'll take you inside the nursery."

Once there, Raina understood why she'd been warned. Several of the newborns were crying, sounding much like screeching cats. Each baby lay in a clear plastic bassinet atop a wheeled cart. "One of your jobs," Betsy said over the increasing wails, "is to wheel them down the halls to their mothers. And this part is very important—make certain you give the right baby to the right mother. Read every bracelet and see that it matches the name on the door and the name posted at the foot of each bed." She pointed to the tiny plastic bracelet looping every baby's wrist. "This is important work, Raina. Don't assume. Know who belongs to whom."

"I'll be careful."

"You leave a baby with its mother for as long as she wants—some are nursing, and the bonding process is important. Check frequently and see if Mom wants the baby returned to the nursery so that she can sleep or eat." Betsy grinned. "Some of these new moms won't get a full night's sleep again for months."

Raina listened closely because she'd never handled a newborn before. The babies looked fragile to her, but Betsy said they weren't.

"Let me show you how to swaddle one." Betsy picked up a crying baby and unfolded the flannel blanket. The baby's legs looked red and spindly and its newborn-sized diaper too large. She laid the baby down and expertly wrapped the blanket tightly around its body. "Now you try it." Betsy handed Raina the baby as if she were passing off a football.

Raina clutched the baby, gingerly laid it down and unwrapped the blanket. She tried to copy Betsy's moves, but the blanket dropped and fell open when the baby kicked.

"Newborns like being swaddled—reminds them of the womb, we're told. Wrap them tight."

Raina tried again and got Betsy's approval. "The hats are cute," Raina said. Each baby wore a little stocking cap in either pink or blue.

"Volunteers knit them. Do you knit?"

"Not at all."

"Well, it seems like you've gotten the hang of swaddling. Here's a chart with names and room numbers. Deliver this row." Betsy pointed to the bassinets holding most of the crying infants.

Raina gulped, hesitant because of her limited training. "I'm ready?"

"You're ready. I'm short-staffed and I need my nurses to do other things. Can you handle it?"

Raina nodded with more confidence than she felt. She walked to the end of the row with Betsy and was about to wheel out the first cart when she looked over and saw a second viewing window. Beyond it was a room with other bassinets holding babies, but these babies had wires and tubes attached to their impossibly tiny bodies, leading to machines surrounding their beds. "What's in there?"

"That's neonatal ICU," Betsy said. "Premature babies, and those born with medical problems and issues, are placed in there because they need round-the-clock intensive care."

Raina found the sight jolting. "They're so small."

"Yes, and some are very sick. But we do everything we can to save them."

"*Do* you save them?"

"Sometimes. Not always."

Raina cast a long, lingering look at the clear plastic egg-shaped bubbles holding the smallest examples of human life she'd ever seen. "It doesn't seem fair."

"Life isn't fair," Betsy said. "Life just *is*."

In October, the weather turned cooler and Kathleen's mother came home. Right before Mary Ellen's arrival, Holly's mother brought over a group of women from her church and they blitzed the house. While the cleanup was happening, Kathleen and Holly hung WELCOME HOME banners and Raina set out vases of fresh flowers. Soon the house smelled of lemon wax, pine cleaner and floral arrangements, and when Mary Ellen arrived, she wept with joy and hugged everybody. Holly cried too, but mostly because Kathleen was moving out of *her* house. "You'll love having your bedroom to yourself again," Kathleen insisted.

"But not my father's undivided attention," Holly said, sniffing. "You were a real cushion between us. It was like having a sister."

Raina handed her a tissue. "Dry up, girl. You

can spend the night at my place whenever you want sisterly company."

Mary Ellen surprised them all by walking through the rooms of her home instead of using her wheelchair. "The therapy helped in lots of ways," she told Kathleen. "I'm determined to be less wheelchair-dependent. Who knows? Maybe I can even get a part-time job and feel useful again."

Carson came over that first night bearing a casserole sent by his mother.

"How thoughtful!" Mary Ellen cried, and invited him to stay for supper.

"Good to see you back in your own space, Mrs. M.," he said.

"I wouldn't be here at all if it hadn't been for you," Mary Ellen told him.

He blushed with pride, making Kathleen love him all the more.

Raina loved her work in the nursery and was grateful to Sierra for giving her the responsibility. She quickly learned that it was the choicest volunteer spot in the hospital, and that only the most trusted and capable teens were chosen for it. She spent all her free time at the hospital, working far beyond the requirements of the Pink Angels program. And why not? Between Hunter's school and work, she saw less of him than she'd imagined.

She was curled up on her sofa with a book on a Saturday night when her doorbell rang. Startled, she glanced at the grandfather clock in the corner and saw that it was after midnight. Vicki was in Orlando at an overnight seminar for nursing supervisors, and Raina was under strict instructions to have no one over. She padded to the door, flipped on the outside light, peeked through the peephole and was shocked to see Hunter.

In the glare of the harsh light, she saw that his cheek was cut and bleeding and his shirt was ripped. Quickly she unlocked the door and jerked it open. "What happened? Are you all right?"

He stood staring at her for a moment, his eyes round with anguish.

"Come inside." She tugged his arm, hauling him into the foyer. A blast of chilled wind followed him. She saw now that his hand was bleeding across the knuckles and looked swollen. "Hunter, please! What's wrong?"

"I've been in a fight," he said.

"You? A fight?" *Impossible!* Hunter was the most nonaggressive person in the world.

"Over you," he said. "Do you know a guy named Tony Stoddard?"

six

A HAND, cold as ice, seemingly squeezed Raina's heart, and the world stopped spinning.

"Do you know him?" Hunter repeated his question, this time more insistently.

"We went to middle school together."

Hunter rocked back on his heels. "So he said."

"Tell me what happened, Hunter. Start at the beginning." She didn't want to hear but knew she had to.

"This Tony and two of his friends came into the restaurant about half an hour before we were closing. They got some burgers, sat in a corner until the place cleared out. Finally, my manager went over and told them they'd have to leave so we could clean up and lock the place down." As Hunter talked, he rubbed his raw knuckles. "It was my night to close and after I finished, I went out to the parking lot. Tony and his friends were waiting for me."

"Did he jump you?" Fury surged through Raina. "Because if he did—"

"No. He told me he wanted to talk to me. He said he'd heard you and I were dating and I told him we were. Then he got this look on his face, this disgusting look, and he—he asked me how I liked . . ." Hunter stopped, clearly unable to repeat Tony's exact words. "I told him to shut up, but he started saying all this stuff about you. Really rude stuff. So I decked him."

She fell silent, the poignancy of the scene stamped in her mind. Hunter, like a knight in shining armor rushing to his girl's defense, because that was just who he was—her defender, the protector of her honor.

"He shouldn't have said those things about you," Hunter said.

"Then what happened?"

"We wrestled. He tore my shirt. I got in a few more hits. His friends grabbed me and held my arms so that he could finish me, but my manager came out. I'd forgotten he was still inside. He yelled at them to let me go and leave or he'd call the police. Tony and his buds split real quick. I told Bill I was all right and I drove straight here."

"You're cut," she said, reaching to touch his cheek.

He dodged away. "I've got to know if what he said is true. Did he 'have' you, Raina? Did he 'do' you?"

Her heart twisted, but she looked him

squarely in the eye. "Yes," she said. Her lips felt like blocks of wood.

"Did he, you know, attack you?"

"No."

His face looked white and pinched like she'd thrown him a body blow and knocked the wind out of him. "In the *eighth* grade? When you were only *thirteen?*"

"He said he loved me. I—I thought he loved me." She blinked back tears. "Back then being popular meant everything to me. Tony was the most popular guy in our school and he—he asked me to go out with him."

"And you just gave yourself away to that jerk?"

She couldn't bear to look Hunter in the face anymore. She stared down at the tiled floor. The normally straight lines looked squiggly and smudged. "He told me he loved me more than anything and when I was thirteen, I believed him. I was stupid."

The ticking of the nearby grandfather clock sounded like cannonballs thudding against the walls of a fortress. All the memories of that terrible time came flooding back to her, threatening to sweep her away and drown her. "He didn't love me, of course. In a couple of weeks, he took up with a sixteen-year-old girl from another school. She had a car and she was cool, while I was . . ." She remembered the words Tony had used as clearly as if he were standing in front of her, slinging them at her again. "I was 'boring,' 'clingy,' 'easy'—'used goods.' He didn't want to waste his time on someone who would 'go down for anyone who asked.' " Her gaze flew to Hunter's. "But there were no others. Just him. I felt humiliated and . . . and dirty."

Hunter sagged visibly. He shook his head. "You were a trophy."

"You could say that."

The silence between them felt as heavy as a lead blanket. Hunter turned and reached for the doorknob. With his back to Raina, he asked, "Were you ever going to tell me? Or were you going to let me go on believing you were . . ." He stopped.

"Pure?" she said, with bitterness. "Well, I'm not. Now you know." She waited for him to say something, anything, but he didn't. "What now?" she asked.

"I don't know. I need some time to think."

Wrong answer, she thought.

He opened the door and stepped out into the cold. The wind scattered a few dry, dead leaves across the floor. He shut the door and Raina stood looking at the wooden barrier while the leaves lay like brittle pieces of her heart around her feet.

Holly was getting a jump on a history paper and was surfing the Web for information about the

Crimean War when she heard Hunter come up the stairs and shut the door of his room. On impulse, she got up and knocked.

"Go away," he said.

She opened the door anyway and stuck her head inside. "That's not very sociable. What if I'd been Dad . . ." Her voice trailed off when she saw his cheek and bloodied shirt. "What happened?"

He began to unbutton his shirt. "I said, disappear."

"Kiss my butt." She came inside and shut the door quietly. "What's going on? Tell me, or I'll wake the dead."

"I had a run-in with some sleaze named Tony Stoddard."

Holly stiffened. "Oh." She reached backward for the doorknob, but Hunter was across the room before she could get it open.

He put his hands against the door on either side of her shoulders, trapping her. "Hold on. You know about him and Raina, don't you?"

"It happened years ago."

"But you knew and you never told me."

"You should go talk to Raina about this."

"I *have* talked to Raina."

Holly's knees turned to jelly. "You did? When?"

"I went to see her after Tony and I mixed it up in a parking lot."

"What are you going to tell Dad? He's

going to go nuts when he finds out you've been in a fight."

"You leave Dad to me. Right now, I want to know why you never told me about Raina and Tony."

Holly peered up into her brother's face. The gash looked superficial, but it was red and swollen. His expression was angry and condemning. "Raina's my friend. And friends don't tell each other's secrets."

"But I'm not just anyone. I'm your *brother*. I suppose Kathleen knows too."

"She's also Raina's friend."

He hit the door hard with his fist, making her jump. He pushed away, paced the floor. "What a cozy little conspiracy! You knew how I felt about Raina! You knew! And you said nothing. Thanks a lot, Holly."

She wanted to make him understand. "Listen, Hunter, friends keep secrets for each other. When you two started dating, I was glad for both of you. You don't know what Tony put her through. Just to be mean, he spread lies and rumors about her. It was awful. She couldn't wait to get out of middle school and leave that crowd behind. And when we heard that Tony had moved during the summer before high school, we were jumping for joy. But then he came back this year and he's been lying in wait for Raina ever since.

I'm glad you punched him." She paused. "You did slug him, didn't you?"

Hunter stopped pacing. "I slugged him, but this isn't about Tony. It's about Raina. And you too, for never telling me about him and her."

"Well, excuse me for being loyal."

"Your loyalty should have ended at our front door. It's not right, Holly. You should have told me."

"It wasn't my story to tell. It was between you and Raina, so don't try to lay a guilt trip on me." She didn't understand why Hunter, who was usually so quick to forgive and who prided himself on doing the right thing, wasn't grasping her explanation. What was so hard? She was glad Hunter had hit Tony—Tony deserved it—although it was totally out of character for Hunter to get into a fistfight.

Hunter crossed to his bed and jerked the covers to the floor. "Go away, Holly. Leave me alone."

"Don't throw me out. We should talk about this. Raina's the one who got slammed."

He ignored her, went to his desk and jerked open his Bible. "I told Pastor I'd lead the youth service in the morning, and I've got stuff to do."

"You sure you're up to such holiness?" He glared at her, and she felt bad about the dig. "You want some concealer cream to help hide your cut?"

"No. I'll just say it happened at work. What's one more lie among friends?"

"You really shouldn't be taking this so hard. It's not the end of the world, you know."

"Good night," he said with a forcefulness that closed the subject.

She left his room, still wondering why he was so wounded by something that had happened to Raina a year before he had ever met her.

Holly woke Kathleen the next morning at seven to tell her the news. Kathleen shook the sleep from her brain to listen. "What a creep," she said.

"Who? Hunter or Tony?"

"Tony, of course."

"It goes without saying that Tony's a creep, but I'm mad at my brother for acting like I did something terrible because I kept my mouth shut. You'd think he'd be proud of me for being a good friend."

"You'd think," Kathleen mumbled, sleep still making her groggy.

"Mom's calling us to breakfast, then we head off to church, so I can't call Raina until this afternoon."

"I'll call her a little later."

"Call her now. From the sound of it, I'm sure she didn't sleep a wink after Hunter left."

seven

KATHLEEN REALIZED that Holly was correct the second she heard Raina's voice, which sounded thick and raspy, like she'd been crying. "You all right?"

"Not really."

"Holly told me what happened. I can come over if you want."

"Don't," Raina said. "Mom will be home about three and I've got to pull it together before I face her."

"What are you going to tell her?"

"I don't know yet. I never told her that Tony has moved back and is in our high school, because she would have freaked."

"You're Queen of Denial."

Kathleen felt rewarded when Raina gave a short laugh.

"You know what a fuss she raised to the principal back in middle school. I can't have her fly off the handle like that again. I don't want it all over school."

"Yes, but Tony was out of control and he was smearing you."

"But I'm a big girl now."

Kathleen fluffed her bedcovers while she thought of something encouraging to say. "This is going to work itself out."

"It all depends on what Hunter does."

"Hunter loves you."

"I'm not sure he loves me quite as much today as he did yesterday."

"All because Tony spilled some dirt about you and him? That sounds harsh."

Raina knew she could never explain it to either of her two best friends. She hardly understood it herself. Hunter's assumption had always been that she was waiting for marriage to have sex, just as he was. Now that he knew she wasn't "pure," would he even want her around? She said, "How is it that I hooked up with the one guy who's a morality major?"

She didn't expect an answer, but Kathleen said, "Because you'd already been used and abused by a guy who isn't."

After they hung up, Raina showered and put on makeup. She wanted to look less unhappy when her mother arrived. Raina would have to tell Vicki something, because her mother would know something was wrong as soon as she saw her. She kept hoping that Hunter would call after church and ease her pain, but he didn't. By the time her mother shouted, "I'm home!" from the foot of the stairs, Raina was desperately sad again.

"Did you have a good time?" Raina called back from her bedroom, putting off the meeting as long as possible.

"I actually snoozed through two of the lectures, but the head of nursing for the Mayo Clinic was sensational." Vicki's voice bounced up the stairs in front of her footsteps. She was still chattering when she opened Raina's door. "Anyway, I—Raina! What's wrong?"

"I—I had a bad night. Does it show that much?"

Vicki eased into the room. "You look like you've been crying."

"Good diagnosis." Raina rose from her bed and crossed to the window. She stared down at the parking lot, at the roofs of cars parked in neat rows like waiting chariots. She wanted to run down, jump into one and drive far away. Maybe not come back.

"Tell me," Vicki said.

Raina turned, slumped against the windowsill and began telling her story, but at the mention of Tony's name, her mother recoiled. "He's returned? Why didn't you tell me? If he says one bad word about you—"

"Too late," Raina said. "But I don't care who he talks to about me. Except for Hunter. He told Hunter."

Vicki rolled her eyes. "For crying out loud, Hunter's more mature than that! Isn't he?"

"It was a shock. I don't want to lose him."

"Look, you made a bad choice with Tony. Surely Hunter understands bad choices."

Raina's eyes filled with tears. "I'm not sure."

Vicki looked both angry and exasperated. "That's why I don't like to see you get so involved with a boy. You have too much going for you, Raina. Don't get hung up on some boy and lose yourself. Or your way."

Raina had hoped for more sympathy, more understanding from her mother. She hadn't wanted a lecture about the perils of love and dating. "It's not Hunter's fault."

"Don't defend him. You've always told me he was different. Well, he doesn't seem too different to me. He's acting like a child. You had sex with Tony. It was a bad choice. You got on with your life. He should accept that and not blame you."

"But it *was* my fault," Raina said, her anger rising. "I said yes to Tony."

Vicki studied her with pursed lips. Finally, she said, "What happened with you and Tony is history. You can't change history. But if that kid even *thinks* about bad-mouthing you again, I'll have him expelled."

"They don't expel people for spreading stories, Mom. Especially true ones."

Vicki rushed forward and grabbed Raina by

the shoulders. "You are *not* any of the names Tony called you. And if Hunter's going to hold this against you, you're better off without him. You hear me?"

Her mother's passion shocked Raina. When she'd been thirteen and Vicki had gone to the principal about Tony, Raina had been embarrassed. But now Vicki's vehemence seemed out of proportion. "I'll handle it," Raina said, wrenching free and rubbing her arms, sore from her mother's grip. "It's my problem and I'll handle it. I'm sorry I even told you."

Vicki closed her eyes, took a couple of deep ragged breaths and stepped aside. "Of course you'll handle it," she said quietly, as if regretting her loss of composure. She walked to the door. "I hope Hunter will come around. I hate seeing you hurt." She paused. "For what it's worth, hard work is good medicine for tough times. It's always helped me. Don't sit around feeling sorry for yourself, because it solves nothing."

Vicki closed the door quietly behind her, and Raina stood staring, bewildered, long after her mother had left the room.

Raina took her mother's advice and spent every free minute in the hospital nursery with the newborns. Being around the tiny babies lifted her spirits. They were new and beautiful and cuddly. Although nothing was said, Sierra and Betsy must have sensed that she was hurting. They gave her free rein and asked little of her in the time she spent working beyond her regular shifts.

One afternoon, Betsy told Raina to gown up and follow her. Raina quickly put a sterile paper gown over her clothes, slipped paper booties over her sneakers and a cap over her hair and followed the nurse into the neonatal ICU—a rare privilege. Together they washed their hands with antibacterial soap and put on latex gloves. "Time to feed the preemies," Betsy said.

"Me?"

"You can hold a bottle as well as anyone, and we're short-staffed today. Flu season—please, don't you catch it."

Raina followed Betsy to one of the plastic bubbles, an incubator that held a tiny baby, born too soon. Gauze pads were taped over its eyes, "to protect them from the light," Betsy said. Tubes and wires attached to portable machines ran into the baby's body. A teddy bear had been placed in a corner of the bubble. "This one was born at twenty-six weeks. She only weighed sixteen ounces."

"A pound?" Raina could hardly believe it.

"She's made progress over the last six weeks— three pounds—and once she gains another, we'll be able to bottle-feed her. When she hits five pounds and gets an 'all's well' from her pediatrician, her parents can take her home."

Betsy led Raina to other incubators, where other premature babies lay, and showed her how to lift and hold one in a nearby rocking chair and how to feed him with a bottle that looked doll-sized. "Don't be afraid of them. They're tougher than they look. And don't let them fall asleep without finishing their formula. Thump them on the bottoms of their feet if they doze off." Betsy smiled. "That's it. Hey, you're good at this. You've got five babies."

"Thank you," Raina said.

Betsy shrugged. "You're my best student."

Holding the babies calmed Raina. They were so small and helpless and they needed her. Well, maybe not *her* exactly, but they needed the care and food she offered. She hummed to them, offering each one a special song. She cuddled every baby, kissed each forehead and traced their tiny features with her finger, a finger that looked gargantuan beside their miniature hands. She already knew that newborns thrived on being held and touched, that without such touching, a baby seemed to wither and dry up.

Grown-up girls need touching too, she thought. Hunter hadn't called her in more than a week and she missed him terribly. She longed to feel his arms around her. She missed the way he toyed with her hair and the way he rubbed the small of her back when he held her. Hunter was a toucher, and she thrived on it. Their separation was a physical pain that nested inside her almost every minute she was awake.

The baby in her arms had emptied the bottle, and Raina held him to her shoulder and gently tapped his back. Tears blurred her vision. Although she and Hunter saw each other in the halls at school and spoke, there was a wall between them that she couldn't breach. "He'll get over it," Holly had told Raina confidently. "I mean, it's not like you cheated on him or anything." But Raina knew that in Hunter's mind, that wasn't necessarily true. He felt betrayed, not so much by what had happened in her past as by his dreams of what could have been theirs and now never would be. *The first time. The first one.*

The Harvest Ball was coming soon, right before Halloween, marking the end of football season. So far, Hunter hadn't mentioned their going together, and naturally, if she couldn't go with Hunter, she wouldn't go at all. No one at school had picked up on their estrangement yet, but if he asked someone else, everybody would know something was wrong.

As she lowered the baby into his incubator, his little hand caught on the necklace Hunter had given her for her sixteenth birthday. She gently untangled the baby's fingers, shut the plastic lid and fingered the heart-shaped pendant with a diamond chip at the heart's tip. Nestled inside the heart was a cross bearing a second diamond chip. "The two most important symbols in my life," he'd said when he'd first fastened it around her neck.

On November twenty-fifth, she'd turn seventeen. With or without him.

eight

"HUNTER AND RAINA broke up? Are you kidding?" Carson stopped chewing in midbite and stared at Kathleen across the table in the pizza parlor.

"I didn't say that. I just said they were having serious problems." Kathleen poked at her slice of pizza, suddenly not hungry.

"That guy's crazy about Raina. They'll work it out." Carson resumed eating. "What happened?"

"I guess it's no secret now." Kathleen told him briefly about Raina and Tony.

"And Hunter's pissed at Raina about something that happened before they even met?" Carson shrugged. "Seems unfair."

"You'd have to know Hunter better. He sets the bar high. I think it's because he's religious."

"I know religious people, and they don't write off someone for things that happened before they ever met that person."

"Holly says he's more hurt than mad." Kathleen plucked a black olive off the slice of pizza and put it aside on her plate.

"Holly doesn't seem that way. She comes across as kind of wild and crazy."

"She struggles with keeping all the rules, but deep down she's got a lot of faith. She's told me that Hunter is thinking about going to seminary someday and becoming a minister."

Carson grimaced. "That would be the last thing on my list."

"Don't you believe in God?"

"Sure. Mom goes to mass every week. Me and Dad, not so much. But then I don't want to be a priest either."

"But ministers can marry. Priests can't."

"Oh, yeah, that's right." He grinned impishly at Kathleen.

"I'm being *serious*. Raina's my best friend and I hate seeing her hurting this way. She spends every free minute at the hospital and she hardly sleeps. She's got bags under her eyes and she's lost weight. I feel sorry for her. Tony is such a creep! Why did he have to say something to Hunter in the first place!"

"Whoa," Carson said. "Back up. This wouldn't have been a problem if she'd told Hunter before Tony did."

"And exactly *when* does a girl tell her boyfriend something like that?"

"The minute things get serious." He eyed her. "Is there something you want to tell me?"

Kathleen felt her face turn beet red. "No!"

He winked and grinned. "I figured that out the first time I kissed you."

She threw a wadded paper napkin at him and hit his cheek. "Excuse me for being so inept."

He laughed and caught her hand, and she struggled to break his hold. "It's okay. You were a fast learner." He stood, came around the table, bent down and kissed her full on the mouth. Three girls at the next table giggled. Carson turned and bowed, saying, "She loves me."

Furious because she felt embarrassed, Kathleen said, "He's conceited enough to think *every* girl loves him."

One of the girls said, "I don't even know him and I love him." The others laughed and waggled their fingers at Carson.

Kathleen crossed her arms and slouched in her chair. "Are you through giving me a hard time?"

He sat back down and leaned forward, his expression serious. "I only do it because I care," he said. "For the record, I think Hunter's making a mistake. But it's *their* problem. You can't fix what's broken between other people no matter how much you want to. They have to work it out."

Carson was right, but it didn't make Kathleen feel less sorry for her friends or resent Tony any less.

*   *   *

"Do you know what's going on between Raina and your brother? And don't say nothing, because I know something's wrong. They didn't go to that dance last week." Evelyn stood in the doorway of Holly's bedroom.

Startled, Holly looked up from the scrapbook she was working on. "The ball is highly overrated. If I hadn't been on the committee, I wouldn't have gone either."

"You're avoiding my question, Holly. Something's happened, and I want to know what it is."

"It's not like I'm Hunter's mother-confessor, you know." There was no way that Holly would divulge the facts.

"But Raina tells you everything."

Holly was going to have to tell her mother something. "One of Raina's old boyfriends has reappeared, and Hunter's jealous." Not the whole truth, but not exactly a lie either.

Evelyn looked thoughtful. "That may not be a bad thing. I think Hunter's far too serious about Raina, anyway. They both should date others. I don't want them getting into trouble."

Which was her mother's unsubtle way of saying, "*I don't want Raina getting pregnant.*" The attitude washed over Holly. "Well, Raina loves only Hunter. The old boyfriend is a jerk."

"That's not a nice thing to say."

"Trust me. It's true."

"Why do you kids think that you have to

have boyfriends and girlfriends, anyway? What- ever happened to just hanging out together?"

Holly would have laughed but didn't think it was a good idea. "I'd answer you, but with- out the experience of having a boyfriend—" She shrugged without finishing.

Evelyn sighed. "I know you think your father and I are too strict with you, Holly, but it's for your own good. Kids grow up too fast these days. And every star in Hollywood seems to think that having a baby without a husband is the thing to do. Your father and I dated three years in college before we married."

Holly suppressed the urge to groan. Her par- ents had attended a small denominational college where they'd met and fallen in love. She'd heard the story many times and thought it hopelessly sentimental, even syrupy. "But how did you know Dad was the one if you didn't date other guys?"

"We didn't need to date hundreds to know quality when we met it," Evelyn said. "All a lot of dating gets you is confused. And dating when you're too young to make good judgments is a huge mistake."

The implication was that Raina had made a mistake and now it had returned to haunt her. Her mother probably thought it was Raina's payback. The attitude annoyed Holly. She still thought that nothing excused Hunter for treat- ing Raina like an outcast. She said, "Mistakes should be forgiven, especially when a person says, 'I'm sorry.' At least I think they should."

Her mother crossed her arms and looked hard at Holly. "In other words, you're not going to tell me what's happened between Hunter and Raina."

Holly smiled sweetly. "Isn't keeping a confidence part of being mature? I mean, you and Dad are always telling me to grow up."

Looking annoyed, Evelyn pushed away from the door frame.

"Why don't you ask Hunter?" Holly called as her mother walked off.

"I have," she tossed over her shoulder. "And he says, 'Nothing.' In my opinion, your confidence-keeping is more like a conspiracy of silence."

"Susan Delano, head of pediatric oncology, is asking for you to work on her floor," Sierra told Holly on the first of November. "You up for it?"

"You bet!"

"You sure you don't mind?"

"Why should I? I worked there a lot last summer."

Sierra shrugged. "It's just a difficult floor, that's all. Nurses experience burnout up there all the time because seeing children suffer is hard to take day after day."

"But we're *helping* them," Holly said, unsure

of what Sierra was getting at. "I don't mind. I can handle it."

"All right. Then take your pager and go check in with Susan."

Returning to the floor brought back summer memories of five-year-old Ben Keller, Holly's favorite patient. He came from a family who lived too far away from Parker-Sloan to stay with him there around the clock. His mother had also been experiencing a difficult pregnancy and was confined to bed rest at the time, so Holly had taken on the child as a personal project, staying with him during his often difficult chemo infusion treatments until he achieved remission and was released. Watching him leave for home that past August had been one of her proudest, if not saddest, moments.

She checked in with Susan. "Have you heard anything about Ben?"

"On this floor, no news is good news," Susan said.

"I was hoping you'd say that."

"Another relapse means big trouble for him, though."

"Wouldn't his doctors just give him more chemo?"

"Not necessarily. Some of those drugs are really hard on a child's system. Especially the heart."

This was news to Holly. "I didn't know."

"You sure you want to stay?" Susan asked.

"Yes," Holly answered quickly. "I want to help."

"Then you've come to the right place, because we need it." Susan smiled. "Go to room five sixteen and meet Tashauna. She's three and had a chemo treatment this morning. Try to get her to eat a little something."

The little girl looked adorable. Tashauna had a head full of black curls, and a pink bow tied around every one. Her brown eyes stared up at Holly from her crib, where she huddled in a corner, her arms wrapped around one of the hospital-issued teddy bears. Holly introduced herself and asked, "Would you like some ice cream?" Ben had loved ice cream, and Holly had always seen that he got some after every chemo treatment.

Tashauna nodded, and Holly got a small cup of vanilla, lowered the side of the crib and offered the child a spoonful. Tashauna ate it and went on to eat every spoonful Holly gave her. Her big chocolate-colored eyes never left Holly's face, and Holly cooed and encouraged her over every bite. When the small cup was empty, Holly praised the child for eating all of it. "Would you like me to read you a book?" she asked.

Tashauna nodded again. Holly got a book, lifted the little girl into her lap and sat in a nearby rocking chair. Tashauna sat very still while Holly read every word of the story with great enthusiasm, using different voices. She was finishing when Susan stuck her head through the open doorway. "Did she eat?"

"Every bit," Holly said with satisfaction. "It wasn't hard at all."

"That's good—"

But Susan was cut off when the child let out a retching sound and disgorged the entire contents of her stomach onto Holly's lap. Holly gagged at the smell and sight. Susan rushed forward, grabbed Tashauna and carried her into a bathroom, where she continued to throw up.

Holly made it to the bathroom and threw up too. She wiped off her clothes with a wet towel, flushed the toilet and returned to the room, where Susan had changed Tashauna into a fresh gown and put her back into bed. The little girl had never even cried.

Embarrassed, Holly offered a shaky smile. "I've always had a weak stomach. Sorry."

"Are you sure you're up to this?" Susan asked.

Holly wasn't sure, but then she felt Tashauna reach through the bars of her crib and pat her shoulder in sympathy. Holly's heart melted and her doubts evaporated. "Maybe I should have started her with a little cola."

She must have made a funny face when she

said it, because Tashauna looked up at her and smiled.

"I think you made a friend," Susan said with satisfaction. "You're a natural, Holly Harrison. A *natural*."

nine

"HOLLY, what's the difference between limbo and purgatory?"

Raina's question caught Holly off guard. Holly was sitting cross-legged on the floor of Raina's room, painting her nails garish shades of blue and green. "Are you writing a paper?"

"Do you know? I figured you might because you're religious." Cold November rain fell outside, and Raina had wrapped herself in an old quilt. Raina used to go to Holly's house; however, lately she felt awkward showing up there, even when she knew that Hunter wouldn't be home.

"I'm not Roman Catholic."

"Do you know?"

"Purgatory is a place where souls go after people die, to suffer and pay for their sins before getting into heaven. Limbo is where lost things end up." She scrunched her forehead. "A long time ago, people believed that babies who died were put in limbo because they hadn't had time to sin and qualify for purgatory. Why do you ask?"

Raina looked at her incredulously. "You actually *know* the difference?"

Holly reddened. "Why did you ask, if you didn't want an answer?"

Raina hugged the quilt more tightly. "I was just trying to figure out which place I was stuck in, limbo or purgatory, that's all. From the sound of it, I'm in both. Is that possible?"

"My brother still hasn't made up with you?" Holly put the caps on the bottles of polish and blew on her nails.

"Not really. Oh, he's polite to me, especially at school, but we haven't had a date since—oh, since . . . you know."

Holly frowned. "Don't think I haven't had words with him about it either. But he tells me to go away, it's none of my business. As *if*! Mom tried to grill me about the two of you the other day."

Raina straightened. "You didn't—"

"Of course I didn't. What kind of a friend do you think I am?"

Raina took a stuffed animal that Hunter had once given her and wrapped it inside the blanket with her. "I should hate him for the way he's treating me. Except that I don't. I wish I did. I wish I could."

Holly hurt for her friend. "Maybe that's what real love is. Not hating someone when you have every reason to."

"Love stinks."

"So let's change the subject. How's it going down in the nursery with all those babies?"

Thinking of the babies made Raina smile. "They're really cute, but they sure can make a racket. Just hustling them back and forth to their mothers makes me realize how much work it must be to care for a baby. I mean, one end or the other is always going off—crying, spitting up, pooping."

Holly laughed. She had told her friends about Tashauna throwing up on her the day it had happened, and she could only imagine what Raina's days were like. "You still want to be a nurse?"

"I like the idea of helping people. Of making sick people better. How about you?"

"I like helping too, but I don't know if I want to make a career out of it. If you could see those little kids on the cancer floor . . . That chemo stuff is pretty grim."

"Well, it's a safe bet that Kathleen won't go into medicine. She turns green if you even say the word 'blood' or 'vomit.' "

"We sure don't see much of her since she hooked up with Carson."

Raina agreed.

"I'm glad for her, though. She really likes the guy. I think everything would be perfect if that nasty Stephanie would fall off the face of the earth."

"I used to think that about Tony too. But

people like him and Stephanie don't go away. They exist to cause trouble. It's their purpose for living."

The girls fell silent as Raina's thoughts returned to her painful separation from Hunter and the memory of what had caused it. Rain splattered against the window and thunder rumbled from far away, reminding Raina of lost souls trapped in purgatory, waiting for blessed release.

On Friday night, Holly stood outside Hunter's bedroom staring at the line of light coming from beneath his door, silently debating whether or not to knock. For once Hunter wasn't at work—the restaurant was undergoing some renovations—and their parents had gone out for dinner and a movie, which meant she and Hunter were alone in the house.

She made up her mind and rapped on his door.

"I'm busy," she heard him say.

She took a deep breath and barged inside. "Too busy for me?" She smiled brightly, hoping he wouldn't say the obvious—"*Yes.*"

He was hunched over his desk and a short stack of papers, which he hastily turned facedown. "There's a reason my door was closed. Is there a problem? Is the house on fire?"

"No problem. Except that we never talk anymore."

"What do you want to talk about?"

"I think you know—Raina."

He glanced away. "That's private, Holly."

"She's hurting, Hunter."

"And I'm not?"

"But you have control of the situation. You can fix things."

"What am I supposed to fix?" He looked sad.

"She can't change what happened back in eighth grade—"

He interrupted. "Do you really think that's what it's all about?"

"Well . . . isn't it?"

"That was just the key that unlocked the door, little sister."

"What door?" Now she was confused.

"The door of my *life*," he said, as if speaking to a child. "I'm thinking about the rest of my *life*, not the past."

"You're eighteen; you've got a hundred years ahead of you."

"I've got college in the fall. Then—well—I'm thinking very hard about going to seminary."

"You're *serious* about being a minister?"

"It's no secret." He sounded annoyed. "I've told the whole family this before. I actually *like* the Church and want to preach the Gospel."

Holly bristled. "And I don't? Is that your point?"

"It isn't about you."

"So what's your point?"

"Raina doesn't," he said quietly. "I went and

fell in love with a girl who doesn't care a flip about religion, who doesn't even believe in God. That wasn't very smart of me, was it?"

His words sobered Holly, gave her pause. Raina had never made it a secret that she wasn't into the "religion thing." She was never unkind about it, but she really didn't believe the way Hunter and the rest of their family did. Holly silently turned over Hunter's dilemma and realized that there were no easy answers. "But if you love each other . . ."

"Love can't solve this kind of problem." Hunter tipped his desk chair onto its back legs, balancing his weight. "And don't forget the problem of earning a living as a minister," he added. "Not an occupation known for its high pay scale. How can I ask Raina to sacrifice the things she might want in life if we aren't of like mind? I've talked this over with Pastor and he's told me how he struggled to get through seminary and make do in his first jobs with a family. It was tough. But at least his wife believed in what he was doing. They were a team serving God."

Holly thoughtfully considered what Hunter was saying. She didn't want to make him angry, but she knew she had to help him see the situation through Raina's eyes. "I don't think you should worry so much about money. Raina wants to be a nurse, so that would help out. And I understand about the other part too. What I don't understand is how you can do all this thinking and deciding and never once talk to Raina about it. I mean, you owe her a conversation about this, don't you think? At the very least, you owe her that."

Sometimes Raina's birthday fell on Thanksgiving, sometimes on either side of it, but it always fell when school was out for the holiday. This year, her seventeenth birthday fell on the Friday after. She was glad to be free from school because she didn't want people to make a big deal out of it. She didn't feel like celebrating. She even told Kathleen and Holly that she and her mother were going to celebrate quietly together and asked them to please hold off on making a big fuss.

"What about our presents to you?" Kathleen had asked.

"Just you and Holly come over Sunday afternoon and we'll go to a movie."

Holly had complained, "You're going to wait *two extra days* for presents?"

Even Vicki had urged her to do something fun on her special day, but Raina said she'd rather stay home, so Vicki baked a small cake and decorated with a few balloons tied to Raina's dining chair. Raina and her mother were just sitting down to dinner at six o'clock when the doorbell rang.

"Probably the next-door neighbor," Vicki said. "She'll want to borrow something. Will you let her in?"

Raina went to the door, opened it and saw Holly, Kathleen and Carson standing on her doorstep. "Happy birthday!" they shouted in unison.

"I said Sunday—"

Holly grabbed one of Raina's arms, Kathleen the other, and they began to drag her out the door. "This is a kidnapping," Holly announced.

"Kidnapping is against the law," Raina said, dragging her feet.

"Okay, then, it's an intervention," Kathleen said. "Either way, you're coming with us."

Raina tried to pull away. "I'm having supper with Mom." She appealed to Carson. "Help me out."

"I'm just the wheelman," he said with a shrug.

Holly glanced over Raina's head and waved with her free hand. "Hi, Mrs. St. James. We're kidnapping Raina, but no harm will come to her unless she puts up a fight."

"No problem," Vicki said, throwing Raina's coat over her daughter's shoulders from the hall rack. "Just remember your curfews."

The girls hustled Raina into Carson's car, stuffing themselves into the backseat on either side of her, wedging her in. "I protest," Raina said, but by now she was laughing because it was both silly and endearing.

"Drive!" Kathleen ordered.

Carson hit the gas.

Raina threw up her hands. "Okay, I give up." She looked at Holly and Kathleen. "So where are you taking me?"

"To Party Central—my house," Carson answered from the front seat. "Mom and Dad are out and we have the place to ourselves."

Raina suddenly envisioned a surprise party. "No one else will be there, right? I really don't want to see kids from school."

"Just us," Carson said.

"You're going to love his house," Kathleen said. "There's an A/V room that will knock you out, and we picked out a stack of movies to watch."

"And cake?"

"Baked it myself," Holly said.

They talked all the way to Davis Island and by the time he had pulled into the driveway, Raina was feeling happier than she had in weeks. She loved her friends for ignoring her request and forcing her out of her self-imposed exile. It had been silly of her not to expect them to do something. They were walking up to the grand brick entrance when the front door opened and a figure stepped outside. "I thought Carson said we were going to be alone," she said to Kathleen.

"We lied," Kathleen said.

The figure stepped forward and pushed back the hood of his sweatshirt, and light from the foyer washed over him.

Hunter. Raina stopped dead.

"Happy birthday, Raina," he said.

ten

HUNTER STOOD with his hands shoved into the pockets of his jeans. His sweatshirt hugged his body and picked up the color of his eyes. A rawhide string bearing a small wooden cross encircled his neck. Seeing him sent a kaleidoscope of emotions tumbling through Raina—shock, anger, fear, desire. She hated him. She loved him.

He held out his hand. She stared at his palm, unable and maybe unwilling to take it. "Please," he said.

She took his hand and it felt so familiar, so perfectly suited to hers that she almost started to cry. Instead she turned to her friends and said, "You set me up."

Carson stood between Kathleen and Holly, his arms slung casually over their shoulders. "He asked if we could help him arrange something special for your birthday."

"We crumbled," Kathleen admitted.

"We're freezing," Holly said, shivering.

"We're going down to the A/V room," Carson

said, ushering them all inside. "You two can have the run of the upstairs." He steered Kathleen and Holly down the hall.

Raina had longed to be with him, but now that she was, she felt self-conscious and off balance. She tugged at her hand locked in his, but he wouldn't let go.

"The living room's this way," Hunter said, leading her to the left of the foyer. "I've had some time to explore while I waited."

"Your car . . . ?"

"I parked around back."

In the huge living room, a lone lamp glowed, casting a pattern of golden light across a long sofa swathed in a soft white fabric. "Nice house," she said, because she couldn't think of anything else to say.

He took her to the sofa but didn't sit. He turned so that he was facing her. She didn't meet his gaze but stared straight into his chest. The heat from his body touched her skin. He smelled of cinnamon and cool mint and fresh laundry. "Happy birthday," he said again.

"You've already said that." She glanced up at him then, made her heart hard. "Nothing's changed, Hunter. I'm still guilty of having had sex with Tony three years ago." She threw the words out like a shield.

"I want to apologize for the way I acted that night. I was mad. I'd just been in a fistfight and my blood was still boiling. And after we talked, I was hurt. No excuse, though. I shouldn't have treated you like I did."

"You could have said this before now. You've seen me every day at school."

"I didn't know how. It was like a snowball—the longer I waited to apologize, the bigger and harder the problem got."

"You were polite to me at school in front of everyone." Her tone was accusatory.

"I—um—I couldn't stand for that creep to think he'd broken us up. That wasn't very fair either."

She agreed. He'd acted petty, but in truth, she hadn't wanted Tony to think he'd broken them up either. "I heard that Tony's dad's been transferred again and that they'll be moving over Christmas break. It doesn't seem fair, you know? He came here long enough to ruin our lives and then he's gone."

"He didn't ruin our lives," Hunter said quietly. "I did."

His admission twisted in her heart like a knife. Their relationship had been fractured, like a glass hitting concrete. The shards lay around their feet and she wasn't sure what to do. "So now what?"

He tucked a piece of her hair behind her ear, and his touch made her heart soften. He still had the power to do that. "Let's sit." They settled onto the plush sofa without touching. She could tell he had something else he wanted to say. Her heart beat faster and her mouth went dry. "Stepping back these few weeks gave me time to think."

"About what?" He was going to break up with her. She felt it in her soul. He had apologized and now he would sever them forever. *Don't cry!* She lifted her chin.

"About what I want to do with my life."

She said nothing, tried to concentrate on keeping her breathing slow and steady.

"I've been offered early acceptance to a small Bible college in Indiana. I'm taking it."

His pronouncement stunned her.

"I've met all my high school requirements, except attendance—you know how they want us in the classroom for X number of days. My counselor, Mr. Dodds, got me a special waiver. I'm leaving right after Christmas."

"Y-you're not going to finish high school?"

"Technically, no. The college has offered me a scholarship. By starting in January, I'll get a head start on the fall freshmen."

"What kind of scholarship?" Her lips could hardly form the words.

"Biblical studies, with a minor in psychology." When she said nothing, he added, "It's a new program for pastoral students."

"You're going to be a *minister?*"

"That's what I'm trying to decide, Raina. I

want to know if it's what I want to do for the rest of my life. I *have* to know."

"And if it is?"

"Then I'll go to seminary after college. It's a long road."

And it was a road that didn't include her. "Holly never said a word to me . . ."

"Holly doesn't know. Only Mom and Dad and a few teachers at school know. I just got my acceptance letter a few days ago."

"But you've been planning this."

"Not for long. The pastor at my church recommended me to the college. It's his alma mater and he hustled things through."

"And what about you and me?" she asked quietly, steeling herself for his answer.

He was quiet, so quiet that she began to think he wasn't going to answer. "Do you know how long I've loved you, Raina St. James? Ever since the first time I laid eyes on you, when you were thirteen." He answered his own question. "Holly used to talk about her friends at the dinner table, but I was a year ahead of her and who cared about my sister's little girlfriends? Then one day, you came over. You were wearing jeans and a tee with pink and blue flowers and your hair was in a ponytail, and you sat on the floor in Holly's room playing Scrabble with Holly and Kathleen."

Raina remembered vaguely. She hadn't gone

over there often because Vicki had kept her in after-school programs when Raina had argued that she was too old for babysitters. Vicki worked long hours, and she'd refused to allow Raina to go home to an empty house. Holly had always talked about her brother, Hunter, but Raina didn't lay eyes on him until she was thirteen. "When I did get to come to your house, you were at basketball practice, or soccer or something."

He nodded. "Plus, I couldn't let my kid sister know that I thought one of her little friends was the most beautiful girl I'd ever seen."

He'd never told her any of this before. "That would have been uncool for sure."

He grinned. "Then you three left middle school and came to Cummings High. Mom made me take charge of Holly that first day. I protested, but secretly, I wanted to be hanging around when she met up with her two best friends. I was grumbling at her about having sister-dork duty when you came through the door and . . . and I thought my heart would fall on the ground at your feet."

Raina remembered every moment of that day, and how hunky she'd thought he was, and how much she'd fought to keep her opinion from Holly. Besides, by then she'd been burned by Tony and had sworn off boys. It had taken Hunter almost the entire school year to finally ask her out, and by then Holly thought it was okay for her best friend and her brother to date. They had been a couple ever since. "And so now it's over," Raina said, holding back tears.

"Not over," Hunter said, clenching his hands into fists.

"You're leaving. I'm staying. What would you call it?" She would break up with him first. Maybe it would hurt less.

"I'll be home when the college semester's over, and I'll work here this summer."

"And then you'll leave again."

"You'll go away to college too."

"Not for another year."

Impasse. They sat side by side on the sofa facing forward, their shoulders barely touching. In the quiet of the great house, Raina heard the faint rumble of a movie playing in the theater room below. Her friends would be expecting a grand announcement about her and Hunter getting back together. They would be thinking that things were going well, that the two who were meant to be together were still together. Fresh tears filled her eyes. She would learn to live without him. She would have to.

Hunter broke the silence with "Can we stay together until I leave for college?"

She shrugged. "If you like."

"I'm not giving up on us."

"You're the one who has to figure things out, Hunter. Not me."

She heard him take a deep shuddering breath. "When I'm with you, I want you. I can't think straight."

She wanted him so badly that she ached. "We should go downstairs. They'll want a full report."

"What should we say?"

"That all's well, I guess. For now. It's what they want to hear. I don't think I can say anything else . . . not tonight."

"All right." He reached behind a cushion on his end of the sofa, extracted a wrapped box and handed it to her. "It's for your birthday."

She'd forgotten it was still her birthday. The fact seemed inconsequential because she was losing the only thing she wanted, the one person she loved. She took the box, beautifully wrapped in silver paper and an explosion of ribbon.

"I had it wrapped at the store," he said, as if apologizing. "I'm all thumbs with paper and tape."

She sniffed, blinked back tears and tore the paper with trembling hands. The box itself was blue velvet, and inside, nestled in a bed of white satin, was an exquisite glass angel, about ten inches tall. "She's gorgeous." Raina lifted the clear figurine from the bed of satin. The angel wore a removable gold halo encircled with small, sparkling jewels.

"The woman at the store said this was numbered—only so many of them were made and then the mold was broken. Those are real Austrian crystals."

"You shouldn't have spent so much money on me."

"I want her to watch over you while I'm gone."

Raina couldn't look at him because her throat ached from the strain of not crying and she was afraid she would lose all composure. She laid the angel back in the box. "Thank you."

He stood and so did she, but before she could take a step, he asked, "Can I . . . would you mind if I held you?"

"I don't mind."

He put his arms around her, pulled her gently to his chest and rested his cheek against the top of her head. She buried her face in his sweatshirt, drawing the scent of him into her very pores. They stood that way for a long time and she wept. When she pulled away, she swiped underneath her eyes and finger-combed her hair. Hunter pulled up his shirt and blotted the moisture off her cheeks with the soft fabric. All she wanted to do was run her hands along his bare skin and make him kiss her until it hurt.

"Ready?" he asked.

"Sure." She put on a happy face for their friends. She and Hunter would give them what they wanted—the two of them together again . . . at least for a few more weeks. She cradled the box with the glass angel, and Hunter laced his fingers through hers. As they walked, she thought about the news video she'd recently seen of coverage following a cataclysmic earthquake. Buildings had been reduced to a pile of rubble and cars had been crushed and turned over like toys.

The images had horrified her, but what she recalled now were the views of the great cracks in the earth around the site. As the world below the surface had shifted, the earth above had cracked apart, and where there had once been solid ground, the surfaces were separated by a chasm. No amount of soil would ever bring the broken halves together again.

Well, Raina's world had shifted and broken apart too. And she could think of nothing that could put it back to the way it once had been.

eleven

"They could have told me. It's not like I don't live in the same house or anything!" Holly was mad and railing to Raina about Hunter's leaving. A week had passed since Raina's birthday and by now it was common knowledge that Hunter would be going off to college right after Christmas. "How can you act so calm about it?"

Raina had just picked up Holly on a cold Saturday morning and they were going to the hospital for an extra volunteer shift. Kathleen had not come with them. "I'm sad about it," Raina said. "And I'm not calm. Whenever I think about it I want to cry, but if I start, I won't stop."

Holly slumped in the passenger seat, crossed her arms and looked sideways at Raina. "Sorry. I didn't mean to go off on you. I should have kept my mouth shut. Dad's always on my case about the way I spout off."

"It's all right."

"Hunter's already packing up and he and Mom are buying stuff for his dorm room. Dad's going to take off work and drive him up. Of course, I'll get his clunker of a car. Not that I can drive it until I turn sixteen in May—" She clamped her hand over her mouth. "I'm doing it again. Sorry."

"It's all right." Only her mother had known the depth of Raina's brokenheartedness. Vicki was amazingly sympathetic; more sympathetic than Raina had ever expected. "I'm so sorry, honey," Vicki had told Raina. "I know it hurts."

Vicki hadn't offered unwanted advice in an attempt to make Raina feel better. Nor had she said dumb mother things like "You're young. There'll be others," or "This will pass. One day you'll look back on this and wonder what the fuss was all about." The only thing she'd said that even hinted of adult-slanted wisdom was "No one knows why, but sometimes you meet the right person at the wrong time. And sometimes you meet the wrong person at a right time. The trick in life is meeting the right person at the right time and being able to know the difference."

If that was true, Raina knew she'd met the right person for herself. She loved Hunter and always would.

"I know Hunter loves you, Raina," Holly said, as if reading Raina's mind.

Raina stared straight ahead, concentrating on her driving. "Sometimes love isn't enough," she said. Holly fell silent, apparently all out of comebacks. If there had been another girl, Raina would have fought like a wildcat to keep Hunter. But how did a person compete with God?

Raina and Holly signed in at the Pink Angels station and made plans to meet for lunch in the cafeteria. Holly zoomed away, eager to get to her little charges on the pediatric oncology floor, but as Raina was attaching her pager to her belt, Sierra stepped into the room. "Oh, good, you're here today. I wasn't sure if you'd come. I have a message for you."

"What's up?"

Sierra handed Raina a piece of pink paper. "A Mr. Charles wants to see you down in Hematology. He left the message late last night. Said he'd be there all day today and then again on Monday. He said it was important."

Raina didn't know Mr. Charles, but the hospital was so big, she wasn't surprised. "I'll check it out."

The blood unit was on the second floor, and on Saturday the area wasn't crowded. She quickly found Mr. Charles sitting behind a desk. When she introduced herself, his face broke into a smile. "Ah, Miss St. James . . . nice to meet you. Edward Charles, chief lab tech."

"Raina. Everybody calls me Raina."

He shuffled papers and found a file folder. "We received a call from Alexandria, Virginia, last night, Sacred Heart Hospital. It appears that you're a possible bone marrow match for one of their patients, a twenty-six-year-old woman with leukemia."

Raina felt confused. "Me? But how—?" Then she remembered that the summer before, Holly had insisted that Raina and Kathleen donate a blood sample to the National Bone Marrow Donor Program because of her favorite patient at the time, Ben Keller. The registry, linked nationally via computers, routinely searched for compatible bone marrow donors and matched them to cancer patients who needed healthy marrow to fight their disease. The odds of being matched were low, but still the registry was a lifesaving tool for patients out of other options.

The man glanced again at the file. "It's your name, all right."

"I—I can't believe it." Holly would have a fit! "What do I have to do?"

"What else? More testing," he said with a grin. "I'll have to draw more blood. You see, we have to look for certain markers in your blood and DNA. The more of these factors that match between a donor and recipient, the better the chances that the transplant will take hold. This first hit alerts the registry that you have the *potential* to be a donor for this particular person. Now we have to match you two more closely and send in the results."

"How many factors have to match?"

"Statistically, unrelated donors have a one in ten chance of having enough matching factors in their blood . . . maybe one in eight on the DNA."

The odds didn't sound all that good to Raina, but still she said, "Well, maybe we'll get lucky. When will I know something?"

"The compatibility testing takes three or four weeks." He studied Raina's paperwork. "First we have to get permission from your parents for me to draw more blood, because you're still a minor."

"Mom will agree. She's a nurse. And she was happy to sign the first form."

"Can you call her? Let me speak to her?"

Raina tracked Vicki down on her cell phone and told her the news. "Amazing," Vicki said. "I'm in a dressing room at a department store at the moment, but I can be over there in half an hour. Just tell Mr. Charles he can draw more blood." Raina handed the lab tech the phone and he chatted briefly with Vicki.

"All set?" he asked after disconnecting.

"Let's go." She followed him into the lab eagerly.

"I wish every healthy person in the country

would sign up for the registry. So many people need bone marrow transplants and without enough donors—well, you know what I'm saying."

"Will I know who she is?"

"There are strict rules about unrelated donors and recipients having contact. You'd have to wait at least a year for a face-to-face meeting, and then only if both parties are willing to meet. It's for the best, you realize. Many things can go awry, and donors feel bad when a recipient dies, so it's best to stay anonymous for a time. Donors do receive a six-week report on the recipient's condition, however."

Raina watched Edward Charles set up the vials and syringes as he talked. Perhaps her marrow could save another's life. Questions swirled through her head, but there was no use in asking any yet. *Maybe* she was a match. It could be a month or more before she knew anything definite.

Kathleen wished she'd never come to the party with Carson. She had wanted to spend New Year's Eve with him alone, but he'd insisted that they hit a huge party at a friend's beach house. The place was crawling with kids from Bryce Academy, and except for Carson, she didn't know a soul. Nor did she want to. Most of the kids were either drunk or well on the way to becoming drunk. Even Carson was drinking beer and feeling little pain. "Are you sure you don't want a beer?" he asked. "Half a beer?"

"I'm the only sober one here, Carson."

"All the more reason."

"*No,*" she said.

He put his arm around her. "You're a girl of principle, Kathleen." He raised his beer can to toast her.

Although he didn't sound as if he was making fun of her, she wasn't sure. "I just don't like the taste of the stuff."

"Never apologize for being a person of principle. Too few of you left in the world." He kissed her.

She tasted the yeasty coolness of alcohol from his tongue and pulled away. "How long are we staying?"

"Aw, come on, honey. It's a party. I don't want to leave until after midnight." He nuzzled her neck. "And I'm going to want to kiss you when that ball drops in Times Square."

She wished she hadn't told him already that her mother had extended her curfew until one a.m. Mary Ellen was assuming that Kathleen and Carson would be at his place, but they weren't, and Kathleen was feeling deceitful, something Carson wouldn't grasp even if she'd told him.

"Hey, there's my buddy, Todd." Carson gestured toward a boy in a blue sweater with his arm around a cute girl in a pink sweater.

"They look adorable." Kathleen's stab at sarcasm seemed lost on Carson. "Listen, I need to use the bathroom," she told him. "I'll be back."

"I'll be waiting."

There was a line at the bathroom door, so Kathleen peeled off and headed outside. She didn't have to use the toilet; she'd only said it so that she could think more clearly. Chilly night air slapped her in the face and she took a deep breath. She heard waves sloshing ashore, driven by a light wind. She squinted at the outlines of mounds atop the sand and realized they were couples stretched out on blankets and covered with more blankets.

Kathleen glanced at her cell phone inside the tiny purse on her shoulder, almost willing her mother to call. However, Mary Ellen rarely called these days because since her surgery, she was feeling much better. She had joined an MS support group and even went bowling once a week! The group met regularly, ate out at restaurants, did holiday projects together. In fact, it seemed to Kathleen that her mother had more of a social life than *she* did. Carson was Kathleen's main diversion, and then only when they both had time between school and her work as a Pink Angel.

Kathleen sighed, zipped her purse and was about to return to the smoke and noise inside the house when she overheard two girls talking near her on the porch. One of them used Carson's name: ". . . don't know why he bothers with her," the girl was saying.

"He could do so much better," said the other.

Kathleen hunched over, wanting to listen but not wanting to be noticed.

"Like *you*, for instance," said the first.

"And why not? I'm prettier than she is."

"Maybe she puts out," mused the first.

"So do *I*," the second girl said.

Both girls laughed as if they'd made a sidesplitting joke. Kathleen felt her face turning red and her temper rising. How dare they talk about her! The girls moved and Kathleen could no longer hear their snide remarks. She waited until they were long gone before stepping back inside the house. She was determined to find Carson and insist they leave. She'd tell him she had a headache. And why not? The two unknown girls were total pains.

The party had grown louder. More people had arrived and the room looked overstuffed. A giant-screen television in one corner of the living room was tuned to the channel showing Times Square, where thousands waited for the dropping of the ball that would usher in the new year. The house reeked of beer and cigarettes. Kathleen shoved her way toward the kitchen, where she'd left Carson and Todd. In the hallway, people milled, waiting in line to reach the beer keg. She elbowed her way past several people, then stopped in her tracks and stared at a couple pressed against the wall in a passionate kiss. Her blood ran cold as she recognized Stephanie and Carson.

twelve

"THANKS FOR picking me up." Kathleen blew her nose and grabbed another tissue from the box stashed in Raina's car.

"I was glad to do it," Raina said. "Sitting home alone on New Year's Eve and missing Hunter is the pits." Two days before, he had left for college with his father, driving a loaded SUV. "You want to tell me what happened? You were babbling wildly on the phone."

"He was *kissing* her, Raina. Carson was *kissing* Stephanie. I couldn't get out of there fast enough."

Raina didn't act shocked or even perturbed. "Did you tell him you were leaving?"

"He didn't exactly look like he was thinking about *me*."

"He might be looking for you."

"I don't care! He's a jerk!"

Raina sent her a sidelong glance. "There might be an explanation."

"Are you defending him? You used to hate him."

"I never hated him and I'm not defending him, girlfriend. I just think you should have pried them apart and demanded an explanation on the spot. You've been dating him for months. And he obviously likes you. I don't see why this can't be worked out—"

Kathleen looked at Raina as if she'd lost her mind. "He was *kissing* another girl."

"I heard you." Raina gripped the wheel hard. Midnight had passed. Lights had dimmed and streets were deserted. The car radio kept playing sentimental music about days gone by. "I miss Hunter," she said softly. "You should fight for Carson if you care about him."

Stricken by the note of sadness in Raina's voice, Kathleen said, "I shouldn't dump on you. You're a good friend and I appreciate your help."

"That's what friends are for." Raina pulled up in front of Kathleen's house, and Kathleen was relieved to see that only one lamp glowed in the front window, meaning that her mother had gone to bed. She didn't want to have to explain her situation tonight. Before getting out of the car, she took deep breaths and told herself to get a grip. She asked, "Have you heard anything about your bone marrow match?"

"I don't expect to hear anything until at least

the end of January. I'm not getting too psyched about it yet."

"You know, Holly's green with envy. She wishes it was her bone marrow that had been matched."

Raina smiled. "She's only told me that fifty times."

Kathleen slid out of the car. "Call me tomorrow. After noon. Way after noon." She shut the door and it made a hollow sound that set a neighbor's dog barking. "And thanks again for the rescue."

Raina leaned sideways. "Don't write Carson off yet. Give him a chance to defend himself."

Kathleen nodded, but the image of him and Stephanie with their bodies molded together burned a hole in her mind. She couldn't think of one thing he could say that would explain his behavior. Not one thing.

Kathleen was roused from a sound sleep by her mother before eight the next morning. Mary Ellen opened the bedroom door and announced, "Honey, Carson's on the phone insisting he speak with you. I told him you were still asleep."

Kathleen sat up groggily. Memories of the night before flooded back. "I'll get it, Mom."

"You'd think that saying goodbye to each other at one this morning would have held him off until later in the day," Mary Ellen mused. "If you want to invite him over for dinner, you can. I'm fixing us a nice pork roast."

Kathleen nodded, knowing she was *not* going to invite him. She'd tossed and turned for more than an hour, unable to shake off the vision of Stephanie and Carson pressed together, before finally falling into sleep. Now that she was awake, the image returned. Once her mother had shut the door, Kathleen reached for the phone beside her bed. "Yes?" she said.

"Where did you go last night?" Carson growled. "I looked everywhere for you when the party started breaking up. I almost called the police, then somebody said they saw you getting into a car with a girl and driving away. Was it Raina? Why did you go? Why didn't you tell me you were going? I've been up all night waiting until a decent hour to call your house, trying to figure out what happened!"

She waited patiently for him to complete his tirade, then cleared her throat. "I would have told you I was leaving except I didn't want to interrupt your lip-lock with Stephanie."

He fell silent.

"Was it good for you, Carson? Because it wasn't good for me."

"Is that what this is about? You think I was kissing Steffie? She was kissing *me*, Kathleen."

"Well, don't I feel stupid? Not to have been

able to see the difference." Her tone dripped with sarcasm.

"She got to the party while I was standing around waiting for you to come back from the *bathroom*—" He poured sarcasm into his answer. "For your information, she was drunk. She was supposed to be in Brazil with her mother, but she showed at the party instead. She came over to me and next thing I knew, she laid a big wet one on me."

"You didn't look to be fighting her off."

"She caught me by surprise. I was in shock—"

"Oh, *puh-leeze*."

"What's with you about Stephanie?" He sounded exasperated. "How many times do I have to tell you that she's a friend and that I'm not interested in her in any other way? When are you going to get over this fixation about her?"

"A fixation? Are you so blind that you can't see that she *likes* you, Carson? That she *hates* me?"

He didn't answer.

"And I'll bet all your friends from Bryce thought it was just so funny," she continued, re-membering the catty remarks of the two girls on the porch. "I can see the headline now: 'Carson Dumps Kathleen, a Nobody, for Stephanie, Right in Front of our Eyes.' When I saw the two of you,

I freaked. I called Raina and she came and got me and drove me home. Maybe I should have told you, but how could I, with Stephanie hanging all over you like a decoration on a Christmas tree?"

He blew out a long puff of air. "You know, Kathleen, one of the things that I've liked about you is that you're a girl who doesn't play head games. Because I hate that about the other girls I know. You're up front and you usually say just what's on your mind. But this vendetta you have against Stephanie makes no sense to me. I've told you what I can about her, and I thought you understood and that things were all right. But they aren't, are they? You just can't let go of whatever it is you have against her."

"What I had against her last night was *her* body up against *yours*."

"All you had to do was walk over and I'd have made it really clear to her that you and I were together, and she would have grabbed somebody else."

"How *flexible* of her. She's a leech." Kathleen was steaming by now.

"I've told you, she's my friend and there's nothing between us. But you don't believe me." His voice had turned cool. "I *hate* playing head games. Especially with you."

She felt white-hot anger pouring through her blood. "Then let me relieve you of the burden of my company!" She slammed down the receiver.

She threw off the covers, jumped out of bed and furiously paced the floor. Before long, what she had just done began to sink in—she'd broken up with Carson. Well, so be it. Who needed a boyfriend who couldn't keep his hands off other girls, anyway?

Kathleen's righteous indignation lasted until late afternoon, when she went to Holly's house. In Holly's bedroom, she told her the whole story and broke down crying. "He made me crazy angry."

Holly handed over a wad of tissue. "Gee, breaking it off seems kind of harsh. He explained what had happened."

"What was I supposed to say? 'That's okay, Carson, whenever Stephanie wants to exchange spit with you, just tell me so I don't walk in on you.' "

"Well, you are awful jealous of her."

"Wouldn't you be? She gorgeous and she's out to get him."

"So you just moved aside. That should make her happy. Now she has a clear path to him."

Kathleen felt annoyed because Holly wasn't more sympathetic. "She's always had a clear path to him. I was just a 'plaything,' remember?" She quoted Stephanie's word when she'd heard that Kathleen and Carson were dating.

"What's Raina's take on all this?"

"I haven't told Raina yet. I told you first."

"Is that supposed to make me feel special? 'Cause it doesn't. It's terrible watching the world fall apart—first Hunter and Raina break up. Then Hunter flies the coop. Now you and Carson call it quits. Oh, wait!" Holly threw up her hands in mock surrender. "*You* called it quits. Carson never got a chance to vote on it. Is that right?"

Kathleen sagged onto the bed, twisting the tissues until they tore. "Okay . . . so I blew up. But you don't know what it feels like to see someone you like kissing someone you dislike . . . and who doesn't like you. And then to have him tell me that I was acting silly and playing games and not being understanding. It hurt, Holly. It really hurt."

Holly sat beside her on the bed. "My dad says it ain't over until the fat lady sings."

"Your point?"

"Maybe you can talk to Carson again and fix things up. He likes you, Kathleen. And I'll bet anything that he's just waiting for you to call him back. Or maybe by the time you get back to your house, he'll have called you."

Kathleen gave Holly a sad look. "My cell's been on all afternoon. He hasn't called."

For Raina, January stretched like a long lonely road and time crawled. Hunter called once, e-mailed several times. He sounded happy. The campus was white with snow, the student center a popular hangout for coffee and endless hours of studying, the classes more exciting than he'd ever imagined. She told him she was glad he was having a good time. And she missed him so much that she ached. She felt left behind, bogged down in high school while he was sprinting ahead into a life she didn't understand.

She found an old Bible in one of her mother's bookcases, dusted it off and flipped through it, hoping to catch a glimmer of the light that beckoned to Hunter so insistently. Some of the stories were evocative, even shocking—King David committing adultery and then having the woman's husband sent off to war to be killed, leaving Bathsheba for himself. Some of the stories were baffling, painful—Job losing his family and all his worldly possessions when God and the devil made a bargain to test his faithfulness. Some of the stories were mystifying, puzzling—a self-proclaimed Messiah telling his followers to "forgive seventy times seven" and to "love one another." Raina didn't get any of it and put the Bible away.

Two things kept her from despair. One was waiting for the results of her bone marrow matching tests. The thought of becoming a donor intrigued and sustained her. To offer another person, a stranger, a second shot at life seemed noble to her and something she wanted to do. The other thing that brought her satisfaction was working in the hospital's nursery. She was a fixture there now and dreaded the day when she'd have to move on to another volunteer job. There was something about the babies that always lifted her spirits.

On the last day of the month, she was gowning up for duty when she saw a lone plastic isolette shoved up against the wall in the neonatal ICU, as if someone had abandoned it. Intrigued, she went through the double doors, gowned up and went into the unit. Inside the bassinet lay a tiny dark-haired baby, covered, not swaddled, with a pale pink blanket. "Who are you?" she asked aloud. The card taped to the edge of the cart read COLLINS, GIRL.

"You shouldn't be in here unsupervised."

Betsy's voice startled Raina. "Oh, sorry. I—I saw this baby parked over here and thought someone forgot to put her back."

Betsy shook her head. "No, she's been put aside on purpose."

"Really? But why?"

Betsy's expression grew pensive, then professional. "This baby was born with a severely compromised liver. A failing liver, actually. She's dying, Raina."

thirteen

"Dying? Can't the doctors fix her?"

"Unfortunately, she has many more medical problems than just needing a liver, even if we could find her a healthy infant-sized, compatible liver—which is extremely difficult. Her heart's missing a valve, she has no spleen, her kidneys are shriveled—well, you get the picture."

"B-but you can't just do *nothing*."

"We're keeping her drugged and comfortable. That's all we can do."

"What about food?"

"We pulled her feeding tube this morning."

Raina was horrified. "I'll feed her! Every hour if she needs it."

"She can't eat. She can't suckle." Betsy touched Raina's arm sympathetically. "And it's her parents' wishes that we don't prolong the inevitable."

"*What?* Her parents have just abandoned her?"

"They haven't abandoned her, they're just letting nature take its course."

"But don't they want to be with her?"

Betsy regarded Raina with gentle eyes. "They're devastated, Raina. Think of carrying a child for nine months and then having her be born with such massive medical problems that nothing can be done to save her. They have other children who need them. Why add to their agony with a bedside vigil, watching her die?"

A lump rose in Raina's throat. The sleeping baby looked peaceful, and her cheeks were plump and round.

"It's fluid buildup," Betsy said, as if sensing Raina's confusion over the baby's seemingly well-fed appearance. "See her skin's yellowish cast? That's from the toxins building in her blood-stream because she has no liver."

"How . . . how long will it . . . take?"

"A few days. I know you think it's cruel, but it's merciful. There are simply too many things wrong with her. Doctors aren't gods." Betsy smoothed the baby's blanket. "Now come on. There are a lot of healthy babies in the other room who need to be taken to their mothers."

"Wait." Raina stared down at the sleeping infant. "Can I hold her sometime? Rock her?"

Betsy considered the request. "That will only serve you, not her."

"I—I just think she should be touched and cuddled." Tears filled Raina's eyes.

"She feels nothing because of the drugs."

"I don't care. She should be more than just some terminal baby shoved against a wall."

Betsy sighed deeply and nodded. "Remember, Raina, all of life is terminal. Healthy or not, we're all going to die. Some sooner than others."

"It isn't fair."

"No, it isn't." Betsy headed toward the door.

"Does she have a name?"

"Annie. They named her Annie."

Raina touched the baby's cheek and hurriedly followed Betsy out of the unit.

For Holly, the hardest thing about Hunter's leaving home for college was that she now became her parents' sole focus. Without Hunter, her buffer zone was gone and everything she did came under scrutiny. She told her friends, "Living with Dad is like living with the eye of Sauron, the dark wizard in *Lord of the Rings*. He sees all, forbids all. I'm going crazy!"

When Holly and her father clashed, her mother often tried to smooth things over. "He loves you, Holly," Evelyn would say. "Don't you understand? He's hard on you for your own good."

"What's so good about wearing skirts below

my knees? I look like an old lady!" Holly ranted. That had been their latest argument from that morning, when she'd tried leaving the house in a cute miniskirt and Mike had made her change.

"Modesty matters," Evelyn said. "You can't go around looking like a tramp."

Holly rolled her eyes. "And I can't go around looking like a fashion refugee either."

"Why is it that you hold what others think of you above what *we* think of you? We're your family and we know what's best for you. You're intelligent, you're attractive—you have so much going for you. Why do you persist in fighting with us over every little rule we give out?"

"Because your rules stink?" Holly ventured a smart answer in spite of knowing it would only get her into trouble.

"That's it. I won't listen to you ridicule all that we believe in. You're grounded," her mother said, leaving the room in a huff.

Holly had shrugged, gone to school and in the bathroom hiked up her skirt to a tolerable length. School and her volunteer job were her escape valves, the two places where she excelled and felt she was taken seriously by adults. Her home life was just something she'd have to endure until she went off to college or moved out on her own.

Raina took Holly to see the desperately sick baby. "That's her," Raina said, pointing through the window of the neonatal unit. "Over by the wall, all alone."

"It's hard to see her. Can't we get closer?"

"No way. I'm not even allowed in there without permission."

"How's she doing?"

"She's hanging on. But Betsy says there's no way she can survive."

"Poor little baby. I hear about kids on the cancer floor who die, but I've never had to see it happen. That would really be tough." Holly looked thoughtful. "Does seeing Annie like this make you sorry you became a Pink Angel?"

"Mom warned me before I signed up last summer that hospitals can't fix everybody and that people die. I knew it, expected it, especially when a person's really old or really sick. But a baby . . ." She shook her head. "I never expected to see a baby die. And I didn't expect the doctors to give up on her so totally. It's like, 'She's broken, can't fix her, let's move on.' "

The way Raina said it made doctors seem callous and unfeeling. "That sounds cold," Holly said. "A lot of the people who work here care. I do. You do. Sierra does. It's a long list."

Raina shrugged. "Mom warned me about getting too involved with one patient too."

"I got involved with Ben, and it turned out okay for him. You need to have faith."

Raina scoffed. "Faith won't heal Annie."

Holly rested her palm against the window's cool, flat surface. She wished she could infuse the element of faith into Raina. It was the thing that separated them from each other, and Raina from Hunter. And while faith might not cure Annie, it would go a long way to help Raina.

Suddenly, Raina plucked her pager from her waistband and peered at it. "My pager went off. Has yours ever gone off?"

"Never."

"Sierra's extension. I'd better call in." Raina grabbed a phone at the nurses' station and made her call. When she hung up, she said, "Sierra gave me another number. She said Mr. Charles has been trying to reach me."

"Maybe it's about the match?" Holly said.

Raina quickly called, identified herself and listened, mumbling a few thank-yous before hanging up. She turned to Holly, her eyes wide with awe. "My test results came back, Holly. I'm a good match for the woman with leukemia. They want to harvest my bone marrow and send it to Virginia in the hopes that it will save her life."

Raina went straight to her mother's office with the news. "Isn't it exciting?"

"I guess so." Vicki looked thoughtful.

"I'm supposed to check with the donor services organization and start preparing for the extraction. I have to watch some videotapes—"

"Wait." Vicki held up her hand. "Let me check into it first."

"What's to check out? I'm a match. We need to get started."

"And I need to know the risks involved for you. No medical procedure is without risks, Raina. I want more information. It's not an un-complicated procedure, you know. They'll stick a syringe into your hip bone. You'll be sore for days."

"But Mom, this woman's already waited over a month for the results of my tests. She could be in serious trouble by now."

"And she has doctors in Virginia to handle her case. So hold on and let me do some home-work. Don't be impatient."

Raina knew she had no choice. Reluctantly, she said, "All right, but let me know the minute you hear something." She bolted out the door be-fore her mother could come up with another sug-gestion that she didn't want to hear.

"I really think it's over," Kathleen told Raina and Holly. They were in the library and taking a study break. "Carson hasn't called once since New Year's Eve."

"Have you called him?" Raina asked.

Kathleen shook her head. "I wouldn't know what to say."

"How about 'I'm sorry'?"

"Couldn't hurt, might help," Holly said.

"I know the two of you think it's so simple. But it isn't. Not for me. If he cared . . ."

"He can't read your mind, girlfriend. Especially from a distance."

"He saved your mother's *life*," Holly said. "Doesn't that make him worth a phone call?"

"Hasn't your mother noticed that he's not coming around?" Raina asked impatiently.

"She asked and I just said we were both busy with school and all."

"I'm sure she bought that," Raina observed dryly.

"I didn't want to spill my guts to my mother," Kathleen said. "Especially now, when life's going pretty good for her. Did I tell you she was dating a guy from her MS group?"

"Your mother? *Dating?*"

Kathleen looked embarrassed. "It's a little weird, but I'm handling it."

Holly tipped backward in her chair, balancing on the back legs. "Well, now it's official. I'm a total loser. When a *mother* can get a date, and I can't . . . well, how bad is *that?*"

"I'm not dating anyone," Raina said quietly.

"And you know my situation," Kathleen added.

Holly glanced from one dejected face to the other. She plopped her chair back down on the floor and grabbed for her books. "Then I guess there's nothing more to do except go eat ice cream." She stood. "You two coming?"

By the time Raina arrived home that evening, Vicki was setting the table for supper. "How's stir-fry sound?"

"We sort of pigged out at the Dairy Freeze, so I'm not very hungry." Vicki gave Raina a furtive glance and Raina knew her mother had something else on her mind. "What is it?"

"I've been talking to people at the hospital ever since you told me about the bone marrow test results."

"And?"

"There's nothing simple about it, Raina. Your life could be at risk, and I can't go along with something that may harm you."

fourteen

RAINA STARED at her mother, shocked by her about-face. "But we talked about this. You said it would be all right."

"No, I said you could sign up for the registry."

"And when I got called, you said I could give another blood sample for the bigger test. Which I did. And which is showing that I could be a donor."

Vicki pinched the bridge of her nose and sighed. "You'll be going under a general anesthetic, and there's always a risk involved when a person goes under a general."

"You're making it sound like *I'm* getting the transplant. And I've always known about going under the general."

"You'll miss several days of school."

"As if I've never missed school before," Raina said, rolling her eyes.

"I'm just not crazy about the idea, Raina."

"But you're a nurse. You understand how hard it is to find compatible donors." Vicki's objections baffled Raina. This wasn't at all what she'd expected, and it made her think there was something going on that her mother wasn't telling her. Raina was puzzling over it when the phone rang. Her mother grabbed it, but after a few minutes of hearing Vicki's one-sided conversation, Raina knew the call was connected to her mother's job. She mouthed, *"I'll be upstairs."*

Vicki said, "Hold on a minute," to the person on the phone, covered the mouthpiece and told Raina, "I've made arrangements for us to sit down with Dr. Portera day after tomorrow so that he can explain everything to us together."

Dr. Portera was a well-known cancer specialist at Parker-Sloan. "All right," Raina said, and Vicki returned to her conversation. Raina went upstairs, still confused by her mother's sudden reluctance to allow her to donate bone marrow to an unknown woman, a thousand miles away. A woman whose last chance might be Raina's healthy marrow.

Raina was restless all the next day at school. She couldn't stop thinking about her conversation with Vicki, nor could she get baby Annie out of her mind. During lunch, she called the hospital from the front office—cell phones were banned during the school day—and tracked Betsy down.

"She's still hanging on," Betsy told her.

The baby had been off the feeding tube three days, and despite knowing that Annie didn't have a chance, every day that she survived gave Raina a perverse hope that she would magically recover. That the God Hunter believed in would somehow reach down and heal the sick and deformed infant. Fifteen minutes later, Raina passed a note to Kathleen in the hall saying that she was cutting out and going to the hospital regardless of the consequences at school.

Once in the hospital, Raina went directly to the nursery but was barred because two infants in the neonatal unit were in crisis and a team of doctors and staff were working to help them. "Come back in an hour," one of the nurses told her. Anxiously, she craned her neck to see if Annie's isolette was in its regular place, and it was. With time unexpectedly on her hands, she wasn't sure what to do. Then she had an idea. Maybe she could get in to talk to Dr. Portera right now and save her mother the time tomorrow.

Up on the floors of the hospital where doctors had their offices, all was quiet, and when she found Dr. Portera's office, there was no one at the reception desk behind the window. Glancing at her watch, she saw that it was one-thirty and realized that many offices closed from noon until two for lunch. Disappointed, she was about to leave when a side door opened and a man poked his head out. "Can I help you?"

"I'm Raina St. James, and I'm looking for Dr. Portera." She held up her hospital ID badge and pointed to her Pink Angels pin.

"You're in luck. Here I am."

"I didn't mean to disturb you—"

"You're Vicki's daughter, aren't you?"

"Yes. Mom and I have an appointment with you tomorrow, but I thought I'd try to meet with you today." She was suddenly embarrassed, realizing that it had been brazen of her to simply drop in on a busy doctor.

"Come on in. I'm just grabbing a bite of lunch and doing some dictation."

She followed him into a large, well-appointed office with leather furniture and a wall lined with bookcases. A half-eaten sandwich lay on his desk. "I—I'm sorry. I shouldn't bother you—"

"No. It's all right. Sit down." He pointed to a wingback chair. "Actually, I was looking forward to meeting you. Your mother explained about your being tapped for bone marrow donation by the registry. I think that's pretty cool." He grinned, as if knowing his wording wasn't doctor-speak.

"Mom was telling me about the procedure. She's concerned about the general anesthetic."

"Sometimes we use a local, but a general is preferred. Let me explain the procedure." He pushed back in his desk chair. "Are you afraid of needles?"

"I don't love them."

"Well, you won't feel a thing. After the donor is out, we put him on his stomach, make an incision on the lower back and put hollow needles into the pelvic bones. Then we attach a syringe and we aspirate—fancy word for suck out." He grinned again. "We collect about a quart of healthy marrow if the recipient is an adult. Once we're finished, we put a bandage over the incision and move the donor to recovery until he or she is fully awake. Sometimes the donor is released the same day; sometimes she spends the night. The donor's sore and stiff, but it doesn't last long. A representative from the National Bone Marrow Donor Program does a follow-up call a few days later. Your marrow will regenerate itself in a matter of weeks, so you'll never miss it."

It didn't sound very complicated to Raina. "And the recipient?"

"Well, the marrow is flown directly to him or her as soon as it's harvested. Believe me, it's more complicated to receive than to give." He picked up a file and flipped it open. "In your case, your recipient is in Virginia. Once the woman is fully prepared, she'll be infused."

"And then?"

"And then we wait to see if your marrow takes hold and reverses her disease."

Raina glanced at her watch and saw that the lunch break was almost over. She could hear his staff rattling around in the hallways. She jumped up. "Thanks for talking to me. I'll tell Mom so that we won't bother you tomorrow."

"It's no bother. I really am pleased that you've agreed to be a donor. What's really fascinating to me is how well you matched this woman."

"Really?"

"I told your mother that it's seldom we get such a good match with unrelated donors. This can mean that the recipient is more likely to not face graft-versus-host rejection as severely. No way to predict, of course."

He'd just told her that her marrow had an excellent chance of making the woman well. "Thanks again," she said, and left his office.

Raina pondered the meeting all the way to the elevator. Funny that her mother hadn't mentioned the compatibility equation. How could Vicki possibly object when the chances of the transplant's working were so good? This wasn't like her mother. No, it wasn't at all like her.

fifteen

RAINA RUSHED to the nursery and saw that the neonatal unit crises had passed and activity was back to normal. She found Betsy and asked for permission to go inside and hold Annie. Betsy looked harried. "You can, but . . ." She paused and looked Raina in the eye. "The end is near for her. Her breathing's shallow and irregular."

Icy fear squeezed Raina's heart. "I—I understand." There would be no miracle for Annie.

Once in the unit, Raina lifted the frail baby from the isolette. She weighed almost nothing, as if her bones were hollow, held together only by bright yellow skin. Raina carried her to one of the several rocking chairs kept in the area for parents to sit in and hold their babies. Most of these babies went home once they had gained enough weight or overcome their medical problems. But not Annie. She would never go home.

Raina held Annie close to her heart and began to rock. The motion soothed Raina. Annie never made a noise. Raina eased aside the blanket that covered the tiny body and saw that someone had dressed her in a buttery-soft pink nightgown decorated with rabbits. One of the nurses, she assumed. Maybe Betsy? Raina slid off the little cotton cap covering Annie's head, exposing her silky dark hair, soft as down. "Poor little Annie," she whispered.

Annie's breath fluttered on Raina's cheek, as delicate as a butterfly's wings. Her chest moved in a peculiar rhythm. *Rise, fall, stop, start, rise, fall . . .* Her lungs sounded tired, as if their work was too heavy, too hard.

Life was abandoning Annie. *So long, it's been good to know you. . . .* She had been born and had lived for a week, three days of that time with only her malformed and barely functioning organs to sustain her after the feeding tube was pulled. Her universe had been these four walls. She had never seen sunlight, felt the wind, smelled flowers or tasted her mother's milk. She was a phantom, a fragment, an almost-being, created and then forgotten by a medical community that could not fix her. To Raina, she was like flecks of sunlight on a garden wall, dancing shadows that flickered as the clouds passed over. She was a flower, stunted and shriveled in its first bloom from a final wintry blast.

Raina was afraid for the baby and realized that it would have been helpful, even comforting, if she herself had a belief in a god or in a timeless place where souls dwell after life on earth. She closed her eyes, willing herself to see beyond the void she believed was waiting for Annie. In her mind's eye, all she saw was Oz—a Hollywood version of a magical setting made solely with colorful lights and beautiful paint.

She thought about limbo, the place Holly had told her about. Was it real? And if it was, could other babies be waiting there? Would they welcome Annie? Shun her?

The fear for Annie's well-being made Raina's heart beat faster like a scary movie or bad dream would, and she wished Hunter were there. He would comfort her, tell her again that the universe was a created place, fashioned and overseen by a benevolent Being. How much she longed to believe that this was so, but she could not. What kind of being abandons the Annies of this life? Or stashes them in limbo, out of the way, out of existence?

A thousand unshed tears filled Raina's mouth. She swallowed them down, smoothed Annie's hair and kissed the papery skin beneath the baby's closed eyes. Annie's breathing had grown sporadic, with longer and longer lapses between breaths. Raina held her own breath, attempting to match the baby's breathing with her own and dreading the moment when Annie would cross over from life into death. Her crossing came softly. *One breath. Long wait. No more.*

In desperation, Raina pulled Annie's lips apart, and, planting her mouth on Annie's, she blew hard. Annie lay limp and perfectly still, and Raina's breath of life evaporated into the air.

She lifted the baby to her shoulder, patted her back and waited until Annie's skin grew cool, until the baby was little more than a doll with stiffening limbs. Raina didn't know how long she sat there like that, holding Annie and rocking her, but at some point Betsy came over and said, "You've been here a long time. Are you all right?"

"Annie died," Raina said.

"Oh, honey, when? Give her to me. She should be pronounced by a doctor." Betsy lifted Annie from Raina's arms. She felt for a pulse.

"What will happen to her now?" Raina asked.

"Her parents will bury her. Our morgue will call the funeral home they've chosen and it will come and pick up her body for preparation, and her parents will grieve all over again." Betsy carried Annie to her isolette and called to the attending physician, who came over and placed a stethoscope against Annie's chest.

Without a word, Raina peeled off her hospital gown and left the area. She went down the hall to a bathroom and was relieved when she found it vacant. She cried until she was empty of tears. She raised her gaze and stared into the mirror. Red, swollen eyes looked back at her.

Mascara smudged her cheeks. She'd thought the darn stuff was waterproof. Didn't anything in this world function the way it was supposed to, the way it was advertised? Mascara shouldn't run if it got wet. . . . Newborns were supposed to live and grow.

She splashed cold water on her face, and patted her skin dry with a scratchy paper towel. She stared at her hands, wiggled her fingers, suddenly grateful and amazed at how well her body functioned. Her heart beat. Her lungs pushed air in and out. The processes were so automatic that she'd rarely noticed them. She turned her hands over, knowing that beneath her skin, millions of blood cells poured through veins and capillaries, carrying oxygen and nutrients to sustain her existence. Her hands held life. *And so did her bones.* She could not have saved Annie. She *could* help save the woman in Virginia with her bone marrow. Raina straightened, tucked strands of her hair behind her ears and headed for the door. She was going to donate her marrow, no matter what her mother said.

Kathleen waited at the end of Carson's street for twilight to engulf the world. This was the problem with driving her mother's huge old wheelchair-adapted van—it was very recognizable and its muffler could wake the dead. She'd wanted to bum Raina's car, something newer and quieter, but Holly had told her that Raina had jumped school at lunchtime to go to the hospital, so Kathleen was on her own with the big ugly van.

She nibbled her bottom lip. Her palms sweated on the steering wheel. "This is stupid," she told herself out loud. "Really dumb." Why couldn't she just pick up the phone and call him and say, "*I'm sorry. I acted like an idiot. Forgive me*"? She lacked the guts. Besides, saying "I'm sorry" over a phone was cowardly. She needed him to see her face and see how sincere she was, and she needed to see his face to gauge how her apology was being received.

"And so why are you waiting?" she asked herself out loud. "Why don't you put your foot on the gas and move this tank of a van down to his house? If you want to apologize, then go do it!" Her stern talk to herself did nothing to quiet her nerves.

She should have brought Holly with her, then remembered why she hadn't. Holly would have *made* her follow through. Holly wouldn't have allowed Kathleen to chicken out.

"Come on," she reasoned. "What's the big deal? What's the worst that can happen?"

He can slam the door in my face. "If that happens, you can get right back in the van and drive home and say good riddance."

Oh, sure. As if I won't be crying like a baby.

"But I miss him. I lov—" She stopped midsentence and amended, "I *like* him. I miss him. I want him in my life."

Taking a deep breath, and seeing that it was completely dark by now, Kathleen put the van into gear and slowly drove forward. In the middle of the block, she remembered to turn on her lights. As she approached Carson's house, she saw that the windows spilled soft light onto the hedges beneath—someone was home. She was about to turn into his driveway when her heart seemed to stop and her blood ran cold. Parked far up in the brick driveway, close to the house, she saw Stephanie's small white sports car. Kathleen froze as the implication sank in and Stephanie's words rang in her ears. ". . . *he finds a new plaything . . . but he always comes back to me.*"

Kathleen pushed the accelerator to the floor and the van shot forward. She didn't slow down until she had crossed from Davis Island to the mainland. She didn't look back. She didn't allow herself to cry until she was home and in the safety of her room.

Raina let herself into the town house and saw her mother sitting at the counter, poring over work she'd brought home.

Vicki glanced up. "I fixed a plate for you to warm in the microwave—Raina? Are you all right?"

"Annie died this afternoon. I was holding her when she . . ."

Vicki hopped off the counter stool. "Oh, honey . . . I'm so sorry."

Raina fended off her mother's hug. "Everybody said she would. It's not like it came as a surprise. I . . . just . . . wish . . ."

Vicki looked sympathetic. "You never forget the first patient you lose. I can still remember mine. He was an elderly man, and so very nice. His wife was shattered. They'd been married fifty-five years. I felt helpless, like 'if there was only more we could do.' But there wasn't. Death is the enemy, Raina. We may keep Death at bay for a time, but he always wins."

Raina heaved her books onto the coffee table. She wasn't in the mood for Vicki's tour down memory lane laced with platitudes. "I went to see Dr. Portera too."

At this, Vicki's eyes grew wary. "Alone? Without me? I told you we needed to go together."

"I thought I'd save you some time tomorrow." Raina's exhaustion and sense of helplessness began to lift. She continued with dogged persistence. "He told me that I was a great match for the woman in Virginia. I wish I knew her name. Anyway, I can't walk away from this, Mom. My bone marrow can help this woman. It might even reverse her cancer and save her life. How can you say no just because I'll be sore for a few days? Or because I'll miss some school? Even the part about me going under a general is bogus. I'm young and healthy and if I needed surgery to fix a problem with *me*, you'd never say a word about the general."

Vicki's expression had turned to stone as she listened to Raina's arguments. "I—I need some time to think."

"What's to think about? Dying woman. Healthy marrow. Transplant ASAP."

Then Vicki surprised Raina by saying the oddest thing. "I'm going upstairs to take a warm shower. Sit down here and wait for me."

"But—"

"Just wait. I'll be down shortly."

Mystified, Raina watched her mother ascend the stairs. A shower? Now? Right in the middle of their conversation? What was going on? Frustrated, she ripped open her book bag and took out her laptop. She set it on her knees and started an e-mail to Hunter. She poured out her heart, weeping as she wrote about Annie, getting irritated as she wrote about her mother's reluctance to allow her to donate her bone marrow. She had just pushed the Send button when she heard Vicki coming down the stairs. Raina set the laptop aside, mentally prepared for another round of arguing her case.

Vicki sat in the wingback chair catty-corner

to the sofa. She was wrapped in her thick white terry cloth robe, her hair wet and slicked back, her face clean and devoid of makeup. She looked vulnerable, younger than her forty-two years. Her feet were bare, her toes painted a bright shade of pink that appeared out of place with the austerity of her expression. She propped both feet on a footstool and crossed her arms. She cleared her throat and said, "Raina, we need to talk."

sixteen

IF VICKI hadn't looked so serious, Raina would have said, "Well, duh! Yes, we do." Instead she nodded agreeably, preparing mentally to challenge anything negative her mother might be about to say. "You start."

"This isn't going to be easy because it—it's going to change your life."

Raina's heart beat faster. What could her mother possibly mean? Suddenly, she had a horrific thought. "Are you okay? You . . . you're not, like, *sick*, are you, Mom?"

"No, I'm not sick."

Raina breathed easier.

"But I'm not all right." Vicki picked at a thread on the arm of the chair. "Sometimes it's necessary to make difficult choices in life. Choices that were right at the time we made them, but that can revisit us years later." Raina bobbed her head, hoping to encourage her mother to get to the point. Vicki sat as still as a rock. "Back in Ohio, when I was sixteen, I was crazy in love with a boy at school. That's why I've always understood about you and Hunter. I knew that you loved him with all your heart."

Love. Present tense, Raina corrected in her mind, not wanting to interrupt but clueless about the point.

"Well, I loved Dustin in the same way—with all my heart. And then—" She glanced at her hands in her lap. "And then just before Christmas of my junior year, I found out I was three months pregnant."

Raina's mouth dropped open. "Pregnant? You?"

"I was amazingly naive. We were having sex, but I wasn't taking any precautions. Dumb, huh? I was playing with fire but expecting not to get burned. And the idea of STDs never entered my mind. We were in love and we were each other's firsts."

When her ordeal with Tony had happened, Vicki had never yelled at Raina or bombarded her with recriminations. She'd brought home a prescription for birth control pills, handed it to Raina and said, "If you're going to be sexually active, don't get pregnant." At the time, Raina had been shocked and relieved, but she had also felt intense shame, knowing she'd disappointed her mother. Suddenly, the way Vicki had handled things back then made perfect sense to her. "Okay, so you got pregnant. What happened?"

"The whole scene got pretty ugly. Dustin's parents went ballistic and refused to let us see each other. My parents freaked out and called me terrible names. Everyone wanted me to have an abortion. But I couldn't. I wanted my baby."

Vicki plucked out the thread and rolled it into a ball between her thumb and forefinger. "My family disowned me. Haven't you ever wondered why you've never met your grandparents?"

"I used to. When I was younger, you said they lived in California and it was too far for us to visit. I used to wonder why they never sent me presents or anything, though."

"It's because they don't know about you."

"They don't know about *me?*"

"They were so ugly and mean to me during my first pregnancy that I decided they didn't deserve to know about my second," Vicki said matter-of-factly. "We haven't communicated for years."

Who was this woman in the room with her? Raina wondered. She'd assumed she and her mother had no secrets from each other, but for Vicki to live all her adult life without ever speaking to her own parents . . . "So you had the baby?" The words sounded foreign to Raina.

"I went to a special home for unwed mothers and yes, I had the baby. A girl. I named her Crystal because she was small and pretty and looked as fragile as glass to me."

"And—and Dustin?"

"His family had shipped him off to relatives in Michigan. I got word to him when she was born, but there was nothing either of us could do. Besides, I think that secretly he was relieved. He had a garage band and was having a good time. He didn't want to get married and raise a child." Vicki ran her hand through her hair, now almost dry, and the light from the floor lamp next to the chair highlighted a few strands of gray. "I gave Crystal up for adoption. It was the hardest thing I've ever done, but I was only sixteen. I couldn't raise her alone. I had no support. She deserved better. It was the best thing for all of us." Her voice caught, and for a moment Raina thought her mother might break down. "I was told she went to a good family. As if they'd tell me she went to a bad family. I told the adoption agency I wanted my records left open. I wanted her to be able to find me if she ever wanted to meet me, get to know me. But she never has."

The wistful tremor in Vicki's voice almost made Raina cry. "Maybe it's because she's happy."

Vicki smiled pensively. "Maybe."

Her mother stopped talking and as the silence lengthened, Raina heard the grandfather clock ticking in the hallway and the faucet in the kitchen dripping into the sink. The refrigerator hummed and the central heat cut on. Everything around Raina seemed ordinary. But nothing was ordinary. Not anymore. She saw her laptop on the coffee table and wondered how she could write about this conversation to Hunter. *Somewhere I have a half sister.* Raina stared down at her hands. All the color was gone from them and they felt cold. "Why didn't you tell me this before now?"

"I wanted to tell you many times. I tried. I almost said something when the thing with Tony happened, but you were so hurt, so sad. I just couldn't."

Angry, hurt, Raina jumped up. "Why didn't you tell me when I was five, or six? It would have been easier if I'd known all my life."

"I was trying to keep life and limb together, Raina. It was just the two of us and that was fine with me. I didn't want to think about her. Don't you know how it hurt to pretend she didn't exist? She was born in April, and every April for the past twenty-six years, I've thought of her. But she isn't *my* child, Raina." Vicki leaned forward, her face a mask of pain. "I gave her up. She belongs to another family. But *you* belong to *me.*"

Raina wanted to hit something, or throw something at the wall. She was furious. "So why tell me now? What's so special about *now?*" And then in an instantaneous flash, like pieces of a puzzle falling into place, her mother's story took on fresh meaning. Goose bumps ran up her arms.

"The woman in Virginia . . . Is she . . . could she be . . . ?"

"Yes. She is."

Raina felt as if the wind had been knocked out of her. She dropped to the sofa like a lead weight. "How do you know? The registry's so secretive." She could scarcely get the words out.

"I thought nothing of it when the first hit came and you were asked to send in a second sample. But when those tests came back and so many factors matched . . ." Vicki let the sentence trail off.

Hadn't Dr. Portera told Raina that very afternoon how unusual it was to have so many factors match in unrelated donors? She'd taken it as a sign that she was destined to be this woman's donor. In reality, it was an announcement that she had a half sister.

"When I suspected the truth," Vicki continued, "the registry was more forthcoming, especially once their unrelated donor was, in fact, a related donor."

Raina's head was swimming. How could this be happening? How could she have lived all her life and not known? How could her mother have lied to her for so many years? Wasn't there some law about keeping this kind of secret? It was cruel. It was hurtful. And she'd always thought of Vicki as a best friend!

"But you tried to talk me out of being a donor. Would you have let your own daughter, the other one, not me, *die?*" Raina asked cruelly.

"Stop it!" Vicki slapped the chair arm with her palm. "You go too far, Raina."

Raina snapped her mouth shut and sent her mother a blazing, defiant look.

"Don't you ever say that to me," Vicki went on. "You can't imagine the hell I've been living through in the past few days knowing that one child is needed to save the other."

"But you tried to talk me out of it. You kept harping on me going under a general, and missing school, and it may not work, and—"

"And I had to know that you *wanted* to be a donor, Raina. I didn't want more pressure on you to become one just because you were related to the recipient. You had to make your decision independent of that issue. And you had to be told of the ramifications. Not just for yourself, but for her too. Your bone marrow may not save her."

Raina squared her chin. "I think it will. I want to do it."

Vicki nodded slowly. "All right. I believe you. And now that you know this story, you may as well hear the rest of it."

Raina's reeling emotions spun out of control. "You mean there's *more?*"

"There's more," Vicki said, leaning back in the chair. "Oh yes. There's more."

* * *

Holly lay on her bed staring up at the ceiling and feeling more bored than ever before in her life. She was totally caught up with her schoolwork—in fact, she was several projects ahead in most of her accelerated classes. Sometimes being smart was a curse. She knew that her mother was sitting downstairs, knitting and listening to amazingly boring music, and her father was at his desk preparing for the adult Sunday school class that he would teach later in the week. The television was off because her parents only allowed it to be on a couple of hours a day, and only if they approved of the programming. Truly, hers was the most boring existence on the face of the planet.

It didn't help that Hunter was away. Without his comings and goings, the house felt tomblike. She'd someday get even with him for running off and leaving her to face this monumental ennui by herself. She couldn't wait until she could drive. But when she could drive, her parents would probably ration that time also. To the corner and back? Maybe to the store to pick up milk? She could see her father writing down mileage in a notebook. *"Now, don't dally,"* he'd say. *"It's five point two miles to the store. One traffic light. Three minutes to park. Ten inside the store. Back home. I'll be looking for you."* Holly shuddered. She was a prisoner.

Holly reminded herself that she should be

more charitable toward her father, because life could turn on a dime. Just last week she'd reported to pediatric oncology only to find the nurses' station in turmoil and Susan, her favorite nurse, gone. "What happened?" Holly had asked.

Cheryl, one of the other nurses, had said, "Susan got a call this morning—her father dropped dead of a heart attack. She couldn't believe it. It was totally unexpected. I mean, the man was only fifty-five years old. And he and Susan weren't on good terms either. She was totally shook. Grabbed her things and rushed home to pack and fly out to Denver, which is where she's from."

"He just died?"

"Keeled over at his office desk. He had no history of heart problems." Cheryl shook her head. "Really sad. I feel sorry for Susan. She kept saying, 'Why wasn't I nicer to him? I can't even remember what we were arguing about.' " Cheryl looked knowingly at Holly. "I guess it just goes to show you that life is short and no one knows when the grim reaper will show up for a person."

Guiltily, Holly said a quick prayer, asking God to forgive her for grousing about her own father. Susan's dad was less than ten years older than Holly's.

She sat up. Where were Kathleen and Raina? Neither was answering her phone. She decided to send them an e-mail. Maybe they were doing homework and needed a break. She went to her desk and hit the screen refresh button on her computer. The parental controls warning popped up. She rolled her eyes.

She opened her e-mail program, and the friendly voice told her she had mail. Good. It was the most excitement she'd had in the past two days, she decided. But when she saw the list of e-mails, none was from Kathleen or Raina. And one was from an unfamiliar name: kn-u-cme. *Can you see me. Who's this?* She pondered for a moment, considered lab partners at school, but they had never used this name. She knew she shouldn't open it. Her parents had warned her about opening e-mail of unknown origin because it could contain a virus. But she had a firewall on her machine.

"What the heck?" Holly opened the e-mail.

Hello—
If I could have one wish, it would be to spend one day of my life with you, Holly Harrison. Maybe someday, my wish will come true.
Shy Boy

Holly sat staring at the screen and rereading the message. *Who in the world . . . ?* She revis-

ited the address line, but it revealed nothing except the time it had been sent. Could it be for
real? Should she reply?

Just then, her bedroom door flew open and
Kathleen ran inside and threw herself across
Holly's bed. "This is the worst day of my life," she
wailed.

seventeen

HOLLY FORGOT about the message on her screen and moved to console Kathleen. "What happened?"

Kathleen stammered out her tale of driving to Carson's and seeing Stephanie's car in the driveway.

"You should have called first," Holly said.

"Why? So he could *lie* to me?"

"He likes you, Kathleen. Don't keep throwing up roadblocks."

"Why do you always want to think the best about people? Take off your blinders."

"And why do you always think the worst?" Holly felt her patience growing thin. She had half a mind to call Carson herself and talk to him about Kathleen. Except that Raina would strangle her because she believed that noninterference in friends' lives was a prime directive.

Kathleen sniffed, but Holly saw that she was calming down. "I'm not wired like you and Raina. The two of you are confident and outgoing. You can talk to anyone about anything. I'm just not that way. I'm shyer. I wish I weren't, but I am." She looked as if the confession embarrassed her.

The word "shy" brought Holly back to her mysterious e-mail. She wanted to talk to Kathleen about it, but now wasn't the time. "I know you're shy." Holly sat beside her friend and put her arm around her. "That's okay. You're probably better off, because I charge in like a bull in a china shop"—that was what her mother had often told her—"and Raina speaks her mind too much. But isn't that what helps us all be friends? We're alike, but we're different too."

Kathleen's thick red hair bobbed up and down as she nodded in agreement.

Holly bounced off the bed. "Have you talked to Raina yet?"

"Raina's missing in action. I've left three voice messages on her cell, and her home phone must be off the hook, because it's been busy forever."

"I can't reach her either." Holly frowned. "But I couldn't get ahold of you earlier either."

"I just probably didn't hear my phone ringing in the bottom of my purse. I was preoccupied, you know."

"What if your mother had tried to call?"

"Mom's on a date. While, I, her daughter, am sitting here feeling sorry for myself."

"Pity parties are my strong suit, but I know just what to do to cheer us up. Come downstairs and I'll dish up some ice cream. Mom got some chocolate fudge sauce for Christmas that's to die for. She hides it, but I know where."

Kathleen cracked a smile. "Do you always eat your way to happiness?"

"Whatever works." Holly led the way downstairs toward the kitchen. "Let's try to call Raina again. Maybe she'll want to come over for the pig-out."

Raina's head hurt. Her brain felt overloaded, and she was afraid that if she tried to cram in one more thing, it would explode. She heard Vicki rattling around the kitchen making a cup of tea for herself, taking a break from their long, life-altering conversation. Vicki had promised that there was "more." Raina was uncertain that she could handle "more." She felt like Pandora trying to stuff all the miseries from the fabled box back inside. She was like the Trojans, wishing they'd never pulled the huge wooden horse into their walled city. If she had never signed up with the registry . . . Then her half sister would have little chance of beating leukemia, she reminded herself.

"Are you sure you don't want anything? A cola?" Vicki returned to the chair, balancing her cup of tea.

"No," Raina said. "Just finish."

Vicki sat, joggled the tea bag a couple of times, squeezed it out with the back of a teaspoon and dumped it on the saucer.

Raina realized that her mother was procrastinating. How horrible could the next part be?

"So back to the family history," Vicki said. "After the birth of the baby, I couldn't return to my old high school. The principal didn't want me there—I was a bad influence, you see. But I didn't want to go back anyway. The place seemed frivolous to me. Girls were planning for proms. I was trying to survive.

"Dustin was finishing school in Michigan, so he was gone. My parents refused to speak to me. I had no real friends. I got a job as a clerk and an apartment with one of the other girls from the home where I'd stayed while I was pregnant. My life was awful. I was so miserable, I thought about . . . well, let's just say, it was a dark time for me."

Suicide. Raina knew that was what her mother had been about to say. She sat still, felt the rush of blood through her vessels, her breath pressing against the inside of her lungs.

"Eventually, I took the GED and got my high school diploma. Then everything was pretty much as I've always told you. I got into a community college and landed a job in a local hospital."

Raina had been told this part all her life,

about how her mother had worked her way through college and a nursing program. She'd just never told Raina the other details. The details that totaled the sum of all her parts, that rounded her out, the good, the bad, the ugly. A lapse, Raina thought bitterly. She should have been told all this years earlier.

Vicki sipped her tea. "Eventually, I got into a special two-year program in Norfolk, Virginia, to become a surgical nurse. I lived with three other girls and had a pretty good time. One long holiday weekend, we went into D.C. to rest and relax." She resettled the cup in its saucer. "One of the girls knew of this little club that featured hot new bands, so we went to check it out. And guess who was playing?"

Raina's heart thudded. She knew by the expression on her mother's face what had happened. "Dustin?"

Vicki gave a thumbs-up. "Nine years had passed since we'd seen each other. But it was like nine minutes. And it took me all of nine seconds to know I still loved him. He had feelings for me too. Maybe not love exactly, but he cared. I dropped out of the nursing program, moved in with him and hit the road with his band."

Raina shook her head in disbelief. Her mother? Her sensible, sane, level-headed, stay-the-course mother became a *groupie*? "Are you kidding?"

"Not kidding. But things were different with Dustin. He and his whole band were into the drug scene. I wasn't. We fought a lot. He sometimes didn't come home, or come back to our hotel when we were on the road. He was always off partying. When he was around, we fought and screamed at each other. And then, one day"— Vicki took a deep breath—"I discovered I was pregnant again."

"Me?"

"You." Vicki hunched down, looking like a china doll abandoned in a corner of a playhouse. "But this time, I didn't tell him. I just packed my things, and I left. I went to D.C. because there were hospitals there where I could work and resume my schooling. When you were born, I gave us both his last name on your birth certificate."

"You always told me he left us when I was two. Is he . . . does he know about me?"

"When you were two, I heard through a mutual friend that Dustin had OD'd in a filthy little motel somewhere in Arkansas. I thought the lie about him leaving us was a kinder story for a little girl who used to ask Santa Claus for a daddy every Christmas."

Raina remembered. Growing up, she had longed for a daddy just like Patty Ellen's, the girl who lived next door until Raina was six. Patty's daddy was tall and strong and smelled like freshly cut grass. He used to swing Patty on her play set in the evenings and help Patty ride her little pink bike up and down the sidewalk. If Raina was in her yard, he waved to her and told her she looked pretty.

Now Raina had come full circle, back to the starting place of never knowing her father. What did it matter? He was a druggie, an addict and worse. She felt battered, as if she'd been slammed into a wall. Her mother went silent, letting Raina absorb all she'd been told. Raina couldn't look at her. She didn't want to look at her. How could Vicki have kept these truths from her for so many years? Her brain felt sluggish, but as she fought her way through the fog of comprehension, one nugget began to coalesce. Crystal, the firstborn, was not her half sister after all. She was her full sister, because they'd both come from the same parents. Her mother had repeated her mistakes with the same man, and Raina was just as much an accident as Crystal had been.

"Tell me about my sister. What have you learned about her?"

"Her name is Emma Delaschmidt. She's a teacher. And she's very sick."

"Then we should go to Virginia as soon as we can."

This time, Vicki offered no resistance, and her demeanor quickly became all-business. "I'll

make the arrangements to pull you out of school.
I'll ask my assistant to step in at the hospital
while I'm gone. Do you want to tell your friends
or not?"

Raina considered her mother's question carefully. Kathleen and Holly were her best friends.
She wanted them to know. She wanted Hunter
to know too. "I'll tell them," she said.

"I wish . . . I'm just sorry . . ." Vicki started
and stopped. "I love you, Raina."

Raina stared at her mother as if seeing her for
the first time. This very day she had cradled a
baby in her arms who had tragically died. And
she'd been forced to abandon a family history
that was mostly fantasy. She'd gained a sister but
lost all feeling for her mother. She was numb inside and out. "I want to save my sister," she said
with almost no emotion in her voice. "I'm going
upstairs now. I'm really tired."

"If there's anything—"

"I don't think there's anything left for you
to do. Unless there's something else you need
to tell me. Some other little revelation about
your past."

"You don't have to be sarcastic. I've told you
everything. The whole story."

Raina went toward the stairs like a sleep-
walker without another word to her mother.

* * *

Over the next few days, Raina felt as if she had been cloned. Raina Number One went to school, the hospital, did homework, kept a smile on her face. Raina Number Two packed her bags for the trip to Virginia, grew nervous about the upcoming extraction procedure and imagined what it would be like to meet a sister she'd never known existed. Raina Number One listened to Kathleen's story about finding Stephanie's car in Carson's driveway and heard Holly burble on about the mysterious e-mail she'd received from Shy Boy, and offered them both advice—"Call Carson immediately" and "Reply to the e-mail if you want to know who sent it." Raina Number Two went through photo albums and pulled out old pictures of herself from elementary school—just in case Emma, her sister, might want to see them.

Raina Number One received pats on the back from hospital and school staff about her impending bone marrow donation. "How brave of you," she was told. "How lucky you are to be able to help someone out this way," others said. And when a reporter called from the *Tampa Tribune* asking to write a feature article about her (how did the paper find out?), Raina Number One begged off, said she'd rather wait until it was all over, and the reporter agreed. Raina Number Two chewed her fingernails down to the quick and cried herself to sleep at night thinking about all she was facing. *I have a sister. My father was scum.*

Raina Number One spoke to her mother. Raina Number Two could hardly stand to look at her as every day, the magnitude of Vicki's deception ate away at Raina's heart and mind. She started an e-mail to Hunter many times but always deleted it because she couldn't put it all into words. And she delayed telling Kathleen and Holly until the night before she and Vicki were to fly to Virginia.

Raina invited her friends over for pizza, and once the deliveryman was gone, once the slices were parcelled out on plates and the sodas were poured, Raina Number One leaned back in her chair and said, "I have something to tell you. Something private and not allowed to leave our circle. You can tell your parents, but nobody else. Do you promise?"

Kathleen and Holly glanced at each other wide-eyed, then looked at Raina and nodded.

Raina Number One started the story, but Raina Number Two finished it in a rush of forlorn tears.

eighteen

THE FLIGHT to Reagan Airport should have been a fun adventure, but it wasn't. All Raina could think about was meeting her sister and the family who had adopted and raised her. Vicki must have had a few conversations with Emma's adoptive parents before leaving, because during the flight, she told Raina what she'd learned. Emma was their only child. Her mother, Helen, worked in the Justice Department; her father, Carl, was with the postal service. They had raised Emma in Alexandria, a Virginia suburb of Washington, not many miles from the hospital where she'd been born, and she had lived all her life in the same two-story brick house. Emma had attended Georgetown University, earned a degree in elementary education and taught fifth grade in a local school. She had first been diagnosed with leukemia when she was twelve. She'd undergone chemo, relapsed when she was sixteen, underwent treatments again and had been well until the year before, when it had been determined that only a bone marrow transplant might save her. She was placed in the national registry, and that was when Raina had entered the picture.

It all seemed simple, except for the extraordinary dynamic of Raina's and Emma's being related through a father whom neither had known and a mother whom Raina had grown up with but apparently had not known either. During the flight, Raina studied Vicki covertly and was surprised to see that she showed no emotion about the impending meeting. Probably all her years as a nurse had conditioned her to remain calm and cool. However, Raina wasn't calm and cool. She felt like a bundle of tangled nerves ready to short-circuit. She hadn't slept well in days and found eating almost impossible.

At the baggage claim, Raina saw a couple holding a cardboard sign with VICKI AND RAINA written on it. The couple looked ordinary, the woman tall and thin with dark hair, the man rounder, with steely gray hair. Her heart thudding, Raina followed her mother to face them. Introductions were polite but awkward.

"You look like Emma," Helen said, her blue eyes filling with tears.

Raina smiled, trying to be brave. "I—I'm looking forward to meeting her."

"She's in the hospital," Carl said. "They have to destroy her immune system—"

"Give them a minute to catch their breath,

honey," Helen said, patting his hand. She turned to Raina and Vicki. "We're so grateful to you. Thank you for coming."

Raina swallowed down the lump wedged in her throat.

Vicki said, "I've reserved a rental car and I booked us a room—"

"We'll take care of your room," Carl said, taking the suitcases from Vicki and Raina. "We know the area and we've selected a hotel near the hospital. It's a nice place. And you can walk to the hospital, which might be easier than driving if the weather's good."

They picked up the rental car, and Vicki followed Emma's parents through the heavy afternoon traffic. "They seem nice," she said absently. "She was raised in a good home."

Crystal-Emma had gone to a good home, like a puppy from an animal shelter. Raina wondered how it must feel for Vicki to look at the faces of the people who had raised her flesh and blood, who had given that child an education and had experienced the horror of Crystal-Emma's cancer treatments. She tried to muster sympathy for her mother, for all the years she'd lost with this adopted daughter, but she kept hitting her wall of anger.

Vicki checked them into the hotel. They stashed their bags, then immediately left with the Delaschmidts to go to the hospital. The small talk between the adults sounded forced and phony—conversations about the weather and life in Tampa, and *"How does Raina like school?"* and *"Isn't airport security a hassle these days?"* Yet it ate up time and filled in the awkward silences and helped them to avoid the more difficult questions.

Raina found the hospital, Sacred Heart, as large and complex as Parker-Sloan. The building, a monument of brick and glass, rose against the dull gray sky in sharp relief. She was glad she'd become a Pink Angel, because the place didn't intimidate her with its size and mammoth sprawl. They walked through a Plexiglas-enclosed bridge into a state-of-the-art cancer center named after the granddaughter of a wealthy couple, a child who had died in the sixties, long before many treatments had been discovered.

"Emma's on the fifth floor," Helen explained as they rode the elevator.

Raina's heart beat faster and she fought to remain calm. It seemed dreamlike to finally be nearing the end of the journey. They walked through double doors, past a nurses' station, rounded a corner and entered a room that looked like spring. Bouquets bloomed in glass vases on every flat surface.

Raina saw a woman sitting up in a hospital bed wearing a hot pink scarf around her head. She looked gaunt, but her smile was beautiful and welcoming. "Hello," she said warmly, holding out her hand. "So you're my biological mother," she said to Vicki. "And you're Raina. I'd know you anywhere. We really do look alike, don't we?"

Yes. They really did. Tears welled in Raina's eyes. Emma was as delicate as a flower, her skin almost transparent, her arm attached to an IV and splotched with dark bruises. "Hi," Raina whispered.

"Quite a bonus I'm getting. A donor and a sister. Well, a half sister, at least."

She doesn't know, Raina thought. Who would tell her? Vicki? At the moment it didn't seem important. "I was surprised too," Raina said, careful not to glance at her mother.

"You're lovely," Vicki said softly.

Emma laughed. "I look better with hair. Even my eyelashes and eyebrows have fallen out, but thank you for saying so." She looked Vicki up and down, curiosity seeping through her smile. "I've always wondered who I came from. Mom and Dad"—she glanced at her adoptive parents—"they've always told me I was adopted. Still, I wondered. Not enough to go looking for you, but . . ." She paused, catching her breath after the exertion of speaking. "Can you tell me anything about my father?"

"Yes," Vicki said. "But later. We only stopped by to meet you."

"Yes, later," Carl said, stepping to the bed and pouring Emma a glass of water.

Emma smiled. "I'm always tired. But so what? I've wanted to meet you both ever since I heard we were a match. But of course I couldn't until we knew we were related. Then they said we could meet. So I've been imagining this moment for a long time. When you're lying in bed all day with nothing to do, well, imagination is all you have. Come closer, Raina." Emma's gaze caressed Raina's face. "You're a junior, right?"

Raina nodded, not trusting her voice.

"And I was told that you do volunteer work at a hospital."

"Pink Angels," Raina managed to say. "That's what they call us. My best friends, Kathleen and Holly, work with me."

"I have two best friends—Janie and Heather. We met in college."

"And you're a teacher."

"I love my job. Each one of those kids feels like my own." She pointed to a corkboard hanging on the back of the door. Every inch was covered with letters and messages on all kinds and sizes of paper. Some had stickers affixed, others were decorated with different-colored pens. The papers fluttered like multihued feathers in the air seeping around the door jamb.

"They must really miss you."

"I miss them."

"We should let Raina and Vicki get something to eat." This came from Helen, who stepped forward and straightened the covers around her daughter. The move looked motherly and possessive at the same time. "Your doctors want to meet us here at seven. Please get some rest."

"Of course," Emma said, winking at Raina and Vicki. "Settle in and come back then. You'll like my doctors. And my fiancé, Jon-Paul Franklin, will be here too. I really want you to meet him. He's a wonderful man."

Raina felt a stab of envy. She longed to have Hunter by her side through the upcoming ordeal.

Out in the hall, Carl said, "Helen and I would enjoy treating you both to dinner."

"No, no," Vicki said, looking apologetic. "We should unpack, grab a nap."

Raina didn't want to be left with either the Delaschmidts or her mother. She wanted to be with her sister, but that wasn't an option at the moment.

When she and Vicki were back in their hotel room, Vicki said, "Pick something off the room service menu."

"I'm not hungry."

"It wasn't a suggestion, Raina."

"A hamburger," Raina said, tossing the menu aside, heading for the bathroom. "I'm taking a bath."

"Don't you think you've shut me out long enough? Don't you think this is hard for me too? I gave birth to her, you know!"

Raina didn't answer. She swept into the bathroom and turned on the taps full blast, drowning out her mother's voice.

"I can't get over how much the two of you look like each other," Jon-Paul said that evening when everyone was gathered in Emma's room and waiting for the doctors. "Can I take a picture?" He held up a camera.

"He's a professional photographer," Emma explained. "Every moment is a Kodak moment to him."

Everybody laughed, breaking the tension that hung in the air. Raina had liked Jon-Paul from the moment she'd met him. He was slender, with chiseled features and light brown hair cut shaggily across his forehead. He was coiled energy barely held in check, and a blind person could have seen how much he adored Emma. Raina scooted next to Emma on the bed, and they mugged for his camera. He fired off a series of shots before Raina could blink.

"Now how about you mothers?" He said it so casually that Vicki and Helen moved forward automatically and took their positions on either side of the girls. Vicki caught herself and started to step aside, but Jon-Paul said, "For posterity. Don't move." He raised the camera.

Smooth, Raina thought.

"You too, Dad."

Carl embraced Emma and they turned to face the camera cheek to cheek. Jon-Paul had just snapped off several shots when three men and two women wearing white coats swept into the room. Raina didn't need formal introductions to know this was Emma's medical team. The head doctor, a tall African American named Samson Wingate, shook Raina's hand warmly. "You don't know how much we've been looking forward to this moment. I was amazed when your test results showed you were such a close match to Emma. When I heard you were her actual blood sister, I whooped." The room of people laughed. Dr. Wingate looked too distinguished to whoop.

"We'll need to run more tests, Raina. You'll need to talk to one of our shrinks—just a formality—and we'll put Emma into isolation and begin radiating her bone marrow."

Emma's diseased marrow would have to be destroyed so that Raina's healthy marrow had a chance of taking hold. The doctor continued, "During that time, Emma will be very vulnerable to germs and microbes. That's why she'll be isolated." He was restating facts they already knew.

The days, or perhaps weeks, before and after the transplant would be the most dangerous for Emma. If she didn't reject the new marrow, if she didn't contract any nasty illnesses, she would have a chance of surviving.

"When do you want to start?" Carl asked.

"The sooner the better," Dr. Wingate said. "Tomorrow."

"Not tomorrow," Emma said. All heads turned to look at her. "Not until after this weekend." She laced her fingers through Jon-Paul's.

Jon-Paul said, "We're getting married this Saturday. Right here in this room, and you're all invited. We've already gotten our license and our wedding clothes and lined up a minister."

"Janie and Heather will be bridesmaids," Emma said before anyone else could speak. She looked straight into Raina's eyes. "And I want my sister to be my maid of honor."

nineteen

THE ROOM erupted—everyone spoke at once. Emma and Jon-Paul held on to each other and calmly waited until the uproar subsided. Raina was the only one smiling at them, the only one flushed with excitement. Their decision made perfect sense to her.

"Emma, be reasonable," Dr. Wingate said, his voice rising above all the others. "We've already waited longer than we should have. Your donor's here. Don't put this off."

"I am being reasonable. It's my life and this is what I want."

"I want Emma to be my wife before the transplant," Jon-Paul added. "I can't let go of her any other way."

Helen leaned forward over the foot of the bed. "Please wait until after you're well, darling. We'll throw you the biggest church wedding ever—"

"I don't want to wait, Mother. I want to go

into this married to Jon-Paul. I know what I'm doing."

Raina understood completely. If it had been her and Hunter . . .

"If you'll tell me about the other bridesmaids' dresses, Raina and I will do our best to find something suitable by Saturday," Vicki said, surprising Raina.

Helen turned on Vicki. "Don't encourage this! Who do you think you are?"

"I'm her mother, just like you. It's what she wants. Let her have it."

Carl took his wife's arm and spoke soothingly. "It's all right, Helen. No sense causing hard feelings. We can throw the big church wedding later."

Emma looked at her mother, her eyes misty. "You go buy a pretty dress too, Mom. You're the mother of the bride and I want you to be beautiful. And to be happy for us."

Dr. Wingate closed Emma's thick medical file. "Look, I know when to fold. No one can override a woman who's set her mind on something she wants." His humor eased the tension in the room. "But just a minimum of people in the room, Emma. And I'm declaring myself the best man."

Jon-Paul grinned and nodded.

"And everyone wears a mask. It would be a disaster if you caught anything," Dr. Wingate said, looking at Emma.

"I'll be good," Emma said, flashing him a hundred-watt smile.

Dr. Wingate shook his head in resignation. "Shall I talk to the hospital pastry chef about baking a cake for you?"

"It sounds *so romantic*," Holly said to Raina on the phone with a sigh.

Raina would have thought so too, if it all hadn't been so deadly serious. "She's pretty awesome. And so is her fiancé. The wedding's going to be small and quick, especially if her doctor has any say. But if I were in her place, I'd marry first too. Have you talked to Hunter?"

"Just last night. He was pretty surprised to hear you were in D.C."

"I never told him about Emma being my sister. Every e-mail I wrote to him sounded like a soap opera, so I didn't send them. He doesn't know." Holly was strangely quiet, making Raina think that maybe Holly had told him, but at the moment she didn't care and didn't want to get into it. So what if Holly had told him?

Holly cleared her throat. "So you're going to be the maid of honor. That's neat."

"Emma gave Mom a picture of the bridesmaid dress and we're going shopping. The wedding's at three on Saturday afternoon, so we have a couple of days to find something."

"It must be weird seeing her, knowing she's your sister."

"It's weird, all right. How's Kathleen?" Raina changed the subject. "Will you tell her hi for me? Tell her that I miss the two of you a lot?"

"I'll tell her."

"And how are things at the hospital?"

"Everyone misses you. Betsy and Sierra send big hugs."

Raina thought of the adorable newborns. There would be a whole new crop by now; the turnover in the nursery was rapid and constant. And she thought of Annie. The memory made her sad but all the more determined to help her sister.

Just then, Vicki walked out of the bathroom putting on earrings and motioned for Raina to hang up. "Holly, I have to go," Raina said. "We're heading to the mall. Wish me luck."

"You've got it, girlfriend—fashion colors for the spring are pink and lime green, and chocolate brown too," Holly said in one fast sentence. "In case you wanted to know."

Raina smiled. "Thanks for the info." She tucked her cell phone into her purse and stood. "I'm ready."

"Put on your coat. It's thirty degrees outside. You don't need to get sick before your surgery."

Raina bristled and started to snap at her mother, but she realized Vicki was right. She couldn't get sick and jeopardize Emma's chances. She grabbed her coat and scarf.

Despite the cold, bleak February weather, the department stores were awash in bright, filmy spring fashions, giving shoppers hope that winter's end was imminent instead of more than a month away. Armed with the picture and Holly's advice, Raina was able to find appropriate styles and colors on the racks. Price didn't appear to matter to Vicki, who let Raina try on everything that appealed to her. The salespeople, eager to help, showed off dresses that Raina would never have worn anyplace. In the end, she and Vicki settled on a lovely float of pale pink georgette strewn with soft ivory-colored dots, and with an empire waist. "You look like cotton candy," the saleswoman said, admiring Raina in the dressing room area. "Pearls would be nice with the dress."

Vicki said, "I have pearls."

"I'm wearing the heart necklace Hunter gave me," Raina announced coolly, ignoring her mother's offer and ending the discussion.

When they went to the hospital, she took the dress for Emma's approval. "Perfect," her sister said. Minutes later, Janie and Heather came through the doorway and Emma made introductions.

"Wow," said the very pregnant Janie. "You two are spitting images of each other."

"Emma's hair's darker," Heather said.

"When I *have* hair," Emma said, making them all giggle.

Raina listened as Emma and her friends talked about the wedding, and even though they were in their mid-twenties and married, they reminded Raina of Kathleen and Holly, making her wonder if she and Kathleen and Holly would still be friends in ten years. A wave of homesickness washed over her. Her life back in Tampa seemed far away, almost otherworldly, and the drama of high school term papers, test scores, basketball contests, upcoming dances, parties and who was dating whom seemed irrelevant. This place was the only real one to her now. Her sister's life, the wedding, the harvesting of her bone marrow formed the epicenter of Raina's universe.

She was grateful that the hotel had a pool and an exercise room. She spent every possible minute in those two places when she wasn't at the hospital. Anything was better than being cooped up with her mother in their room. They still weren't talking much because for the first time in Raina's life, she didn't have anything to say to Vicki. She hurt inside. Her heart felt as if it had been scraped and laid raw. How had Vicki allowed the years to slip by without telling Raina the truth? Raina told Emma about Tampa, Hunter and school—but she really wanted to tell her about their father and the fact that they were truly sisters.

"It's your story, Raina, not hers," Vicki said curtly the one time Raina mentioned it to her mother.

"You shouldn't keep it from her. She should know about him."

"She has a father in Carl. Why burden her with another? Besides, she has enough to think about at the moment."

Raina backed off, but she knew that one day when this was all over, she would tell Emma about Dustin St. James.

On Saturday, Raina and Vicki ate lunch in their room while Raina channel-surfed and watched time crawl by on the bedside clock. Two hours before the wedding, there was a knock on their door. Raina leaped to answer it.

"Don't! What are you thinking? Never open the door until you know who's knocking. Look through the peephole first."

Vicki's irritation scraped across Raina's nerves. She peeked through the hole that gave a fish-eye view of the hallway, let out a squeal and jerked open the door.

"Surprise!" Holly and Kathleen chimed in unison. Evelyn, Holly's mother, stood behind them, waving.

The three friends rushed to hug each other. Raina pulled Holly and Kathleen inside the room. "How did you get here?"

"We drove."

"All the way from Tampa?"

Evelyn nodded. "It's a twenty-hour trip, if anyone ever asks. We started early yesterday. Kathleen and I did the driving. Actually," she added dryly, "I brought them to keep Holly from stealing the car and coming on her own."

"It was a plan." Holly grinned. "You didn't think we'd let you go through this all by yourselves, did you?"

Evelyn looked at Vicki. "Plus I figured *you* might need some company." The two women held a silent conversation with their eyes, as only women can.

"Thank you," Vicki said, embracing Evelyn.

Kathleen added, "Mom wanted me to come, but she couldn't. She said it meant the world to her when everybody showed up before her surgery last year. So we ditched our classes and here we are."

"Didn't want to miss out on anything," Holly said, bouncing on one of the king-sized beds.

"We have our own room upstairs," Evelyn said. "They brought plenty of schoolwork to do, so you won't be tripping over us. We thought we'd stay through Raina's surgery."

Raina almost wept with gratitude.

"That would be wonderful," Vicki said. "I know things will go well, but still it's nice to have friends with us."

Raina went to the closet. "Come see my dress for the wedding."

"You can't come to the ceremony," Vicki said to the others, almost apologetically.

"We know. We'll wait here and we'll do dinner, maybe a movie when you come back." Evelyn kicked off her shoes and wiggled her toes in the carpet.

Holly and Kathleen looked at Raina and in unison shouted, "Heated pool!"

Evelyn rolled her eyes. "These three are inseparable. You'd think I'd be used to it after all these years."

Raina caught sight of the clock. "I'd better get dressed."

"You can come up to Emma's floor with us," Vicki said quickly. "Meet Emma's parents and fiancé. She's a pretty special girl."

"I don't doubt it," Evelyn said. "I know her mother and sister. They're both pretty special too."

twenty

EMMA'S HALLWAY had been turned into a wedding chapel by the nurses. White crepe paper hung in streamers from ceiling to floor. Large white and silver paper wedding bells were strung across the entrance to her room. In a spacious private waiting room, a small reception had been arranged. A table was spread with a white cloth and held a two-tiered wedding cake, bowls of nuts and mints, cans of sodas and a big pot of coffee. Music played in the background. Baskets of silk flowers filled the occasional tables. "How beautiful!" Evelyn exclaimed as they entered the room.

A number of guests were already gathered, and all turned when Raina came inside. For a moment no one spoke; then a woman said, "For a minute, I thought you were Emma . . . you look so much alike."

Raina smiled self-consciously and went to stand beside Janie and Heather, dressed in their long mauve gowns. Kathleen and Holly tagged along and Raina introduced them around. Janie handed Raina a small silk bouquet. "She can't have real flowers today. The water can breed germs; silk is safer."

Heather said, "Janie and I had them specially made up for all of us."

Dr. Wingate swept into the room with Jon-Paul, causing Holly to whisper, "He's cute."

"Which one?" Raina whispered back.

"Both of them," Holly said, making Kathleen jab her with an elbow.

"Listen up," Dr. Wingate said. "Only the principals are allowed in the room. Jon-Paul's set up a video camera, so the rest of you can watch on the closed-circuit TV." He gestured toward a big-screen television on the far side of the room. "There's a camera in here too, and Emma will be able to visit with all of you after the ceremony. Just stand in front of the camera and wave, and she'll see you on the TV set in her room."

Raina spied a camera high on the wall in the corner near the table.

"Are we ready?" Everyone murmured, and Dr. Wingate stood in the doorway. He passed out surgical masks to Emma's parents, the bridesmaids and Raina. Raina tied hers around her mouth and nose expertly, for she'd worn masks many times when handling the more fragile newborns. "You too, Mrs. St. James," Dr. Wingate said.

Vicki looked surprised. "Are you sure?"

"I have a list from the bride," Dr. Wingate said, patting his breast pocket and smiling.

They walked down the hall to Emma's room. A minister stood waiting just outside the door. He also wore a mask. Dr. Wingate opened the door and let everyone pass him, single file.

In the center of the room, sitting in a wheelchair, gowned in white and wearing a white satin surgical mask across her mouth and nose, Emma waited. An IV pole on the side of the chair held a bag of clear fluid. The tubing looped to the needle taped to her arm. She wore lace gloves and held a gorgeous cascade of silk orchids, calla lilies and satin ribbon that spilled onto her lap. Her head was covered with a crown of tulle, pulled back to expose her beautiful eyes. White satin slippers peeked from beneath the hem of her gown.

Raina's eyes grew misty and she heard Helen stifle a sob. Janie and Heather took their positions on Emma's left, leaving room for Raina to stand beside the chair. Jon-Paul came quickly to stand on the other side. The minister took his place in front of them both, and Dr. Wingate stepped back to join Emma's parents and Vicki.

Raina had a perfect view. What she saw was a look of pure love in Jon-Paul's eyes, a look of pure happiness in Emma's.

"Who gives this woman to this man?" the minister asked.

"Her mother and I," Carl answered from his place near the door.

Raina's hands trembled and her throat closed up as she heard Emma and Jon-Paul repeat their vows. *"Till death do us part . . ."* The words took on a powerful meaning for her. Most couples married in glowing health, expecting to stay healthy well into old age. Emma and Jon-Paul had no such illusions. Dr. Wingate handed Jon-Paul the wedding band, and he slipped it onto Emma's gloved finger with a promise to cherish her forever. The simple band of gold sparkled more beautifully than any diamond.

With the vows completed, the minister said, "You may kiss your bride."

Jon-Paul knelt in front of the chair, took Emma's hands in his and kissed her softly through both masks, on the backs of both hands and on her cheeks. "I love you," he said.

"Ladies and gentlemen," said the minister when Jon-Paul stood. "May I present Jon-Paul and Emma Franklin."

Emma waved to her wedding party and then to the camera. Raina heard clapping and cheering coming from all the way down the hall. Janie and Heather bent and kissed Emma's forehead, and so did Raina. She caught the heavy chemical odor of the medications and felt a stab in her heart. "Not the best perfume, is it?" Emma whispered. "I was afraid to wear any perfume because

I'm real sensitive to smells, and wouldn't it be gross if I threw up on this beautiful dress?"

"Gross," Raina said.

Raina stepped aside so that others could come up and congratulate the couple. She watched Vicki especially, saw that her eyes were filled with tears. She heard her mother say, "Thank you for letting me be a part of this."

"You gave me life. How could I have not invited you?"

Dr. Wingate called, "Everybody out. There's a party waiting. Let's let the bride and groom be alone for a while." And like a shepherd, he ushered the wedding party out of the room and down the hall while music swelled and nurses tossed handfuls of confetti on them.

"I cried like a baby," Kathleen said over the top of her cola can.

"It was the most beautiful wedding *ever*," Holly said, sniffing hard. "I want one just like it. Except not with the hospital, IV and wheelchair."

"You're so picky," Kathleen teased.

Raina drew patterns across the frosting on her piece of wedding cake with the tines of her fork. She wasn't hungry for the sugary concoction. She felt melancholy. What a way to begin a marriage—facing a bone marrow transplant.

"When's your big day?" Kathleen asked.

"Monday. Dr. Wingate says it won't take too long for the radiation treatments to destroy Emma's marrow. I'll do a couple of days of testing, and when Emma's ready, Dr. Wingate will extract the marrow. While I'm in Recovery, they'll begin infusing her."

"And then?"

"And then I have to go home and we wait to see if it works."

"How long?"

"About a month if there are no setbacks. If there aren't any, she'll transfer to an outpatient care facility where they'll look after her until she can leave. I was told it could take a hundred days before she can actually go home."

"Long time!" Holly said.

"Can we talk about something else?" Raina asked. She set the uneaten cake aside and turned to Kathleen. "How's it going with you and Carson?"

Color crept up Kathleen's neck. "I did something . . . brave. For me, that is. I—um, sent him a big bunch of flowers with a note saying, 'Miss you.' "

Raina grinned. "Way to go, Kathleen! What happened?"

"I don't know. We left to come here the day they were supposed to be delivered."

"I'll bet he'll be waiting on your doorstep when you return," Holly said.

"How about you? Anything new?"

Holly shrugged. "Same old, same old." In truth, she'd received two more e-mails from Shy Boy, and she'd answered the last one. "*Who are you? Can we meet?*" But she'd left town too, so she didn't know if he had answered. For all she knew, it was a hoax, someone's idea of a sick joke.

Just then, there was a commotion at the door and they looked up to see a hospital security guard in the doorway. "What's up?" Dr. Wingate asked as the guests grew quiet.

"I have a kid out here who claims he's one of the wedding party. He's real insistent. I brought him up just in case he's telling the truth."

The guard moved aside and Hunter came forward, looking rumpled and in need of a shave.

Raina cried out, jumped up, knocked over her chair, ran and threw herself into his arms. He locked his arms around her, buried his face in her hair. She began to weep, her whole body shaking with emotion. "You're here! Oh, Hunter . . . you're here!"

"I guess he was telling the truth," the guard mumbled.

"Seems so," Dr. Wingate said.

Hunter kissed Raina's mouth, her eyes, her throat, and she returned his kisses, like a starving person suddenly thrust before a banquet table. She was oblivious to everything except the feel and taste of him, her love, her wonderful love.

And even when Holly and Evelyn came over and hugged them both, neither let go. They just held on tight while the people in the room burst into spontaneous wild applause and camera flashes went off all around them.

twenty-one

THE PARTY was over, and the guests were gone. Raina and Hunter sat alone in the waiting room on a vinyl couch, the remains of the celebration all around them. The lights were low, the music silenced, the door closed for privacy. "How did you know how much I wanted you here?" Raina asked. "Did you read my mind?"

"Because I knew how much I wanted to be here. When Holly told me she and Mom were coming, I knew I had to come too. I finished a paper, told three professors I'd be missing their classes for a few days, borrowed my roommate's car and started driving east. I drove all night."

"How long can you stay?"

"Until you're through your surgery and I know you're all right."

She nestled against him. "I'm sorry you didn't get to meet Emma. I've told her about you, though."

"I'll meet her when she's well."

"Hunter, I'm scared for her. What if my bone marrow doesn't work?"

He smoothed her hair, kissed her forehead. "She's in God's hands."

"He'd better hold on to her," Raina said fiercely.

"It's his specialty."

His faith buoyed her spirits. It usually did. "I've missed you so much." Her voice cracked.

He squeezed her more tightly. "Not as much as I've missed you."

"You've missed me?" She sat up and looked him in the face. "You sounded so busy with college, I wasn't sure."

"Why do you think I stayed so busy?" That made her smile. "I'll be home as soon as the term's over in May. I'll have to work, but we'll have the whole summer together."

The thought warmed her heart. "Listen . . . I want you to know how sorry I am about Tony and all. How sorry I am that—"

He placed his fingers across her mouth. "Shhh. That's ancient history. I'm the one who's sorry that I made such a big deal about it."

"But you wanted me . . . expected me . . ."

"Raina, what happens to a person's body isn't nearly as important as what happens to their heart. The good thing you're doing with the transplant and all, that's what's important right now."

"But she's my sister."

"You didn't know that when you first agreed to do it. You wanted to help her when she was a stranger. You offered your help because that's who you are. And it's just one of the reasons why I love you."

"Still?"

He lifted her chin and looked into her eyes, making her wonder if she would sizzle and melt. He said, "Still and forever."

About the Author

Lurlene McDaniel began writing inspirational novels about teenagers facing life-altering situations when her son was diagnosed with juvenile diabetes. "I want kids to know that while people don't get to choose what life gives to them, they do get to choose how they respond."

Her many novels, which have received acclaim from readers, teachers, parents, and reviewers, are hard-hitting and realistic but also leave readers with inspiration and hope.

Lurlene McDaniel lives in Chattanooga, Tennessee.

A sneak peek at *Holly's Story*, the next book in
the *Angels in Pink* series

one

"IS THERE ANYTHING MORE FAB than summer va-
cation?" Raina St. James's question sounded
more like a declaration. "No classes, no home-
work, nothing to look forward to except weeks
and weeks of sunshine."

Raina and her friends were spending the day
at Carson Kiefer's house, lounging by the pool
under a clear blue sky. Burgers sizzled inside the
mammoth grill on the patio, and the aroma min-
gled with the scents of sunscreen and chlorine.

"I heard the school board wants to have year-
round classes," Holly Harrison said. She was sitting on a towel at the side of the pool painting
her toenails a flamboyant shade of hot pink.

"If they do, I'll shoot them," Carson said.
"We need a break." He took a running leap off

the diving board and cut like a knife through the water. He swam the length of the pool underwater, coming up beside Kathleen McKensie's float.

She opened one eye. "If you splash me, I'll shoot *you*."

"Crabby."

"I've just doused myself with sunscreen and I don't want it washed off." She lifted her sunglasses to look at him treading water next to her. His brown eyes danced and droplets of water clung to his buttery tanned shoulders. "If I didn't burn to a crisp without it, I wouldn't mind," she said. "But *que sera sera*." She resettled the dark glasses on her nose and rested her head again on the cushioned pillow of the float.

He tossed his head and slung beads of water over her body. "Did I get you wet?"

She ignored him.

"Want me to lick off the water?"

Instantly, her face flushed bright red. "Go away."

He laughed. "Maybe you'd taste like coconut."

"Pervert." She wasn't even mildly annoyed. It felt so good to be back with him, to be a part of his life again, she would have tolerated any amount of his teasing. The weeks she'd spent apart from him the past winter after she'd blown up and hung up on him over a spat about Stephanie Marlow had seemed like an eternity.

"I'm, like, so disrespected," he announced. He put his elbows atop the float, leaned over her and ran his cool, wet tongue across her mouth.

Shivers shot up her spine. "Scram!" she hissed.

He laughed, arched backward like a dolphin and dove under the water.

Raina watched, amused, from the circle of Hunter's arms. They were sitting on a lounge chair together, Raina in front, and Hunter was smoothing lotion on her back. The stroking of his fingers was lulling her into drowsiness. He bent forward and nibbled on her earlobe. "He's right about the coconut taste," Hunter whispered.

"I'll buy you an Almond Joy," she mumbled.

"You taste better."

"I'm flattered." Waves of contentment washed through Raina, mimicking the lapping water against the colorful tile sides of the pool. Hunter would be home for the entire summer and she'd be with him every possible minute, between his job at the fast-food restaurant and her volunteer work with the Pink Angels program at Tampa's Parker-Sloan General Hospital. Every possible minute.

"What do you hear from Emma?" Hunter asked, leaning back into the chair and pulling Raina against him.

"I talked to Jon-Paul last night. Emma's

finally home. She was asleep when I called." Raina closed her eyes, conjuring up the faces of her sister and her sister's husband—a sister she had never known existed until February.

"But she's doing all right?"

"She is now." It had been touch and go as Emma's doctors fought to stave off infections that threatened her new bone marrow, but after a hundred and ten days, she had been sent home to complete her recovery and begin her married life, cancer free.

"And you?" He touched her hip where bone marrow had been extracted to save Emma's life.

"You asked me the same thing yesterday. The answer's the same today. I'm fine. Just a small scar."

"Can I see?" He nuzzled her neck.

"I'm shocked you would ask. I mean with all these people looking on."

He laughed. If there was one thing she could trust about Hunter, it was that he wouldn't look even if she stripped on the spot. "I'm not a prude."

"Yes, you are." She twisted around and kissed him lightly. "That's what makes it work between us. I keep trying to jump your bones and you keep pushing me away."

"This will change when we get married."

Her heart did its usual stutter-step. They talked about sex and marriage, but truthfully, huge hurdles lay in front of them. For starters, he wanted to be a minister and had taken early acceptance to a small Christian college in Indiana last Christmas. And she wasn't sure she even believed in God. Only Holly, Hunter's sister, realized the depth of their dilemma.

"And your mother? You forgiven her yet?"

Raina stiffened. The question prickled. "I'm the sinner, you're the saint, remember?"

"Can't hold it against her forever, you know."

"We've reached a tentative peace agreement. I don't mention it. She doesn't have to walk on eggshells. It's not perfect, but it allows us to coexist."

His brow knitted. "I'm not sure it's smart not to talk about it—"

Raina shushed him with two fingers over his lips. "Don't make me get rough with you. Throw you in the pool and hold you under."

"Hey, I can defend myself. I'm the guy who got into a fistfight over you, remember?"

How could she ever forget? Tony Stoddard's mouth had almost destroyed her relationship with Hunter. "Don't joke about that, Hunter," she said quietly. "I don't think I'll ever be able to joke about it."

His arms tightened around her. "I was the idiot, not you."

She knew he wanted to make it up to her for the way he'd treated her after Tony's "revelation," but he didn't need to. She loved him and wanted to be with him forever—yet the hurdles remained.

Carson hoisted himself out of the pool. "I'd better turn the burgers." He padded over to the grill, raised the lid and stared down. "Um—I think they're burned."

Holly went over and confirmed his suspicions. "Hopelessly burned."

"Dad's never burn."

"He stands over them full-time," Kathleen called. She had straddled the float and paddled to the shallow end of the water, where she used the steps to exit the pool. She walked over to the grill.

Together, the three of them stared in dismay at the charred remains of their lunch.

"Too bad. I'm starved," Kathleen said.

Carson turned off the grill and turned to the others. "So how does everybody feel about pizza?" The agreement was unanimous, so he picked up his cell phone and hit a single button.

Incredulous, Kathleen asked, "You have the pizza parlor on speed dial?"

Carson grinned. "A guy's got to eat." He slipped his arm around her.

Holly sidled to one side, feeling as left out as she always did. She'd turned sixteen in May and now had her driver's license, not that it did her a whole lot of good. Her parents only allowed her to drive Hunter's beat-up car, and only when he wasn't using it, which wasn't often. Her emancipation wouldn't go into full effect until he returned to college in September—if then. But it wasn't the car issue that bothered her the most. It was the lack of a boyfriend, a guy of her own, a boy who took her out on dates or came with her when she hung out with Raina and Hunter, Kathleen and Carson.

In mid-May, the e-mails from Shy Boy had stopped as suddenly and mysteriously as they had begun. Her e-mails to him bounced back to her in box, so she was no closer to knowing who he was than when he'd first contacted her in February. She'd printed out all their communications and kept them in a notebook, stuffed between her mattress and box spring, because of course her parents knew nothing about Shy Boy. They never would have approved, so she printed and then erased the messages as soon as they arrived. She'd read them so many times that she could quote them.

> Holly: Are you some 35-year-old pervert, pretending to be sixteen?
> Shy Boy: I'm seventeen, and not a pervert . . . well, I'm not most of the time.
> Holly: Why don't you want to meet me face to face?

> Shy Boy: I know what your face looks like. It's the face of an angel.
>
> Holly: But I don't know what YOU look like!
>
> Shy Boy: My mother thinks I'm handsome.
>
> Holly: I should believe her because . . . ?
>
> Shy Boy: Because mothers don't lie. And because it's what's inside a person that counts, not what's on the outside.
>
> Holly: So . . . are you saying that you have a face only a mother can love?
>
> Shy Boy: My face is decent. Honest. And I only have eyes for YOU.

Then the e-mails had stopped. She felt irritated and impatient with him. And she felt sorry for herself. She finally had a boy interested in her, and he was a phantom. She couldn't see or touch him. Raina had said, "Savor the moments. If he got hold of you once, he'll do it again."

And Kathleen had said, "Remember how long it took me to get it together with Carson. Be patient."

Easy for them to say. They had their guys locked in their arms and their hearts. The only bright spot in Holly's life this summer was the

Pink Angels program. Volunteering at the hospital was what got her out of bed these bright summer mornings. That and the remote possibility that one day soon, she'd turn on her computer and Shy Boy would have sent her another e-mail, this time setting up a time and place for them to meet once and for all.